HIGHLAND CHRISTMAS

EMMANUELLE DE MAUPASSANT

Edited by
ADREA KORE

First published in 2017

www.emmanuelledemaupassant.com

CONTENTS

THE HIGHLAND SERIES

Highland Christmas is the sequel to *Highland Pursuits,*
a romantic comedy, set in London and Scotland, in the 1920s,
featuring defiant debutante Lady Ophelia Finchingfield.

Highland Wedding, Volume Three in the series, is set for release in
late 2018.

DEDICATION

This novella is dedicated to the lovely Ms. Kore, my friend and develop-mental editor, who worked with me to bring the characters of Castle Kintochlochie to life.

Read more about <u>Adrea Kore</u> at the end of this edition, in About the Editor.

CHARACTER LIST

OPHELIA'S FAMILY

Lady Ophelia Finchingfield - our reluctant debutante, lately of
Girton College, Cambridge
Pudding - Ophelia's Cairn terrier
Sir Peter Finchingfield
father to Ophelia, turkey millionaire, and MP for King's Lyppe, in
Norfolk
Lady Daphne Finchingfield - mother to Ophelia, daughter of
Lord and Lady MacKintoch

CHARACTER LIST

CASTLE RESIDENTS - UPSTAIRS

Lady Morag MacKintoch - grandmother to Ophelia (mother to
Lady Daphne)
Aphrodite - Morag's Pekinese
Sir Hector McLean - brother to Morag
Lord Hugo MacKintoch
late husband to Morag
Edward (Teddy) MacKintoch - late son to Morag and Hugo
Lady Constance Devonly - old friend of Morag and Hugo
Hamish - nephew to Constance, working as estate manager for
the Kintochlochie Estate
Braveheart - Hamish's wolfhound

CHARACTER LIST - SCOTLAND

CASTLE RESIDENTS - DOWNSTAIRS

Mr. Haddock - butler
Mrs. Beesby - cook and housekeeper
McFinn - footman
Murray - stable lad
Hettie - housemaid, looking after the linens
Bessie and **Ethel** - kitchen maids
Gertie and **Gladys** - housemaids, with some kitchen duties
Susan - scullery maid
Mary - lady's maid to Lady Morag and to Lady Constance, also
assisting Lady Ophelia

CHARACTER LIST - SCOTLAND

NOTABLE GUESTS AT CASTLE KINTOCHLOCHIE

Horatio Buffington - an artist

Felicité - Hamish's old flame, newly married to the very wealthy Wilberforce Worthington

Wilberforce Worthington - owner of Hollywood's Lionheart Film Studios

Colonel Montague (Monty) Faversham - rather a lecherous old buffer, but newly enamoured of Enid, and promising to mend his ways

Rex - the Colonel's labrador

Enid Ellingmore - a lady novellist of sensational romantic fiction, engaged to marry the Colonel

Marjorie Ellingmore - Enid's sister, a keen animal rights activist

The Reverend Reginald and Mrs. Violet McAdam

Lord Arthur and Lady Mildred Faucett-Plumbly and their granddaughter Flavia

Peregrine Belton - a young man with a passion for motoring

A WEDDING IS ANNOUNCED

NOVEMBER 4TH, 1928

THE MOUNTAINS SURROUNDING Castle Kintochlochie were already well-frosted, but the fire was blazing cozily in the drawing room as Lady Morag MacKintoch took afternoon tea, seated with her granddaughter Ophelia and long-time companion Lady Constance Devonly.

'Oh, how marvellous!' exclaimed Morag, looking up from the letter in her hands. 'Constance! Ophelia! Our old friend the Colonel has proposed to dearest Enid, and she's consented to take him! It's like something from one of Enid's novels, except for the heroine being a little more mature in years.'

'Goodness me! That was quick work,' said Ophelia, licking sugar from her fingers and reaching to receive the pink notepaper from her grandmother.

'Delightfully romantic,' remarked Lady Devonly, taking a sip of tea. 'They were rather love-struck when they set off together for their jaunt to the Lake District, after your lovely sixtieth birthday party, Morag. I did wonder if something of the kind might happen.'

Morag contemplated the array of cakes on the stand. 'About time he settled down. He and Enid seem very well suited.'

'Jolly good luck to them, I say.' Ophelia scanned through Enid's correspondence, tucking a curl of her unruly, dark hair behind her ear. 'Never too late for love, even for an old cavalier like the Colonel. Although I do think it's rather rum that they're cavorting about the Lake District, getting up to all sorts, and Enid totally unescorted. No one would approve of me behaving like that!'

'I know, dearest. I don't suppose the world approves terribly of Enid either, but she's old enough for certain things to go less remarked upon.' Morag reached for an iced fancy. 'Nevertheless, I expect Colonel Faversham has been signing them in as Colonel and Missus, to avoid raising eyebrows.'

'Easy enough to find a ring to pretend with, I suppose,' said Ophelia.

'Yes, dearest.' Lady MacKintoch fed a crumb of fondant to Aphrodite, her beloved Pekinese, who was perched in her lap.

Ophelia's own little terrier, Pudding, was sitting at her feet, licking her lips, eager for a similar treat. However, Ophelia never allowed her sugar; bad for the teeth, and Pudding was excitable enough as it was.

'Will they be heading off to Gretna Green, like eloping lovers, do you think?' asked Ophelia, tearing the crust from a cucumber sandwich and passing it to the dainty lips of Pudding.

'Oh no, darling. Did you not read to the end? Enid asks if they might be married from the chapel, here at Castle Kintochlochie.'

Aphrodite shifted in her mistress' lap, her nose twitching at the scent of almonds, in anticipation of another morsel.

'Neither has many relations to speak of,' sighed Morag, 'Their parents are gone, and the Colonel's only brother was killed long ago, in the Boer War, before he managed to have children. Enid's sister Marjorie is sure to make the journey; her other sibling succumbed to the Spanish flu, years ago, as did Constance's own dear child.' She leaned over to squeeze Lady Devonly's arm. 'Such a terrible illness. No one was safe.'

Constance looked to the window and hid her face in her teacup for a few moments.

'Enid suggests a small party, but I'm sure we can do better,' mused Morag. 'I've already written to your mother, Ophelia, to suggest she and Sir Peter join us. It's been far too long since Daphne visited the estate, and she must be missing you, darling.'

'Top-hole,' said Ophelia, forcing a smile. It had been rather blissful not to have her mother about. Moreover, Lady Daphne might resume in her persistence to see her daughter married. Scotland was suiting Ophelia perfectly well, and she'd no desire to return to London, to be promenaded like a prize cow before a paddock of panting bulls.

'We had such a splendid time at my birthday celebration,' continued Morag. 'I'll invite some of our neighbours, and we might recreate the festivities of the summer. Since it was that event which brought the Colonel and Enid together, it would seem apt.'

'What a super idea!' Constance pressed Morag to take the last of the macaroons. 'I know the Beltons and Faucett-Plumblys are travelling up soon.'

'Utterly bliss-making,' said Ophelia, her teeth clenching at the thought. She'd spent a large part of Morag's party avoiding unwanted attention and had gotten herself in a shameful pickle not long afterwards with young Peregrine Belton. She blushed to think of how she'd attempted to seduce him, when they were out in his car, and how he'd dumped her, unceremoniously, upon the doorstep of Castle Kintochlochie. On the rebound from Hamish, Ophelia's amorous advances had been thrown back in her face. Peregrine had scarcely been able to escape fast enough.

'That's settled then.' Lady MacKintoch beamed. 'Constance, didn't you mention that Felicité is soon returning... from America, isn't it, with her new husband? Wouldn't it be fun to invite them? We need some youthful glamour to offset all the ancient bones.'

Ophelia's fingers tightened on her cup.

'Jolly good thinking,' said Lady Devonly, rising to give the fire a poke. 'When does Enid want us to plan for, Morag dear?'

'She's suggested a Christmas wedding,' replied Lady MacKintoch, popping a stray raspberry into her mouth. 'Isn't it exciting!'

HOOKED

DECEMBER 12TH, 1928

OPHELIA HUGGED herself beneath the blanket and buried her hands deeper in her pockets. It wasn't cold enough for the lake to freeze yet, but that time wasn't far off. The twilight sky was just the right colour for snow.

She watched Hamish pull against the tension in the fishing rod, his forearm thick, sinews straining.

'Incoming!' The trout flung skywards, silver scales glinting, mouth gaping. 'It's a beauty!' he declared. 'Sunrise and sunset: always the best times for landing trout.'

She bent to look it in the eye and the fish gave a sudden flip-flop, making her veer back, almost losing her balance. Hamish's arms were around her waist, steadying her, before she had a chance to tumble.

'Steady there. Don't want you going overboard again.'

It wasn't long ago that she'd fallen into the loch from his boat, wearing little but her best silk dressing gown.

'I'm quite alright, no need to fuss.' Ophelia found herself feeling annoyed.

He smiled, taking a seat in the narrow rowing boat, and bidding her lean back against his chest. The smell of woodsmoke and sweet sweat assailed her, stronger than the tang of trout, as he wrapped his arms about her. Ophelia's desire overcame her irritation and she wished he might reach beneath her clothes. His hands were always full of heat.

'You're too cold for this,' he said, rubbing her back. 'We'll head in.'

Only a few months had passed since Hamish's return from Edinburgh, released from his entanglement with Felicité, after her impulsive flit to America. Ophelia remained indignant: on that summer evening in the cabin, it was fair to say she'd been as willing as he. They'd desired one another in equal measure, but Hamish hadn't been honest with her. Not honest enough to share the nature of his commitment towards Felicité; not until afterwards. Ophelia had spent too many nights mulling over those events, unable to decide how far he was worthy of forgiveness and how far he deserved her anger.

Since then, it seemed almost every night she'd lain awake, waiting for the handle to turn, for him to slip in and join her. Twice, in the luxuriance of her bed, having made love, he'd suggested that they formalize things, but he hadn't gone down on one knee. She wasn't sure that she wanted him to. It might change things, and weren't they just fine as they were? Hamish knew how to take precautions. If she did end up 'in pig', he'd marry her, she knew.

A soft mist was blurring the hillside as they drew up alongside the jetty, and Hamish secured the ropes.

'Great news about Enid and the Colonel.' Hamish helped Ophelia step out. 'Although they're an unlikely pair: the sensational lady novelist and the whisky-soaked old buffer. Rather inspiring though, seeing love burning bright, despite time bringing the candle low.'

He pulled her close and bent his mouth to whisper. 'We might suggest a double ceremony. I've no grand title to offer you, and we'd remain here, of course, but you'd be my wife. No more skulking down corridors.'

She twisted against the tickle of his breath on her ear, then relaxed, allowing herself to submit to the tightening of his embrace.

'I might rather like your night-time prowling,' she answered, raising her lips for a kiss. 'There's nothing clandestine about the marriage bed.'

'Wicked girl,' Hamish chided, laughing into her hair.

She felt the familiar wave of jealousy, battling her heart's desire to give herself to him without fear. The thought of having that French vixen back under the roof of Castle Kintochlochie made her feel quite nauseous. It would take all her self-control not to throw a cup of hot coffee into Felicité's lap.

They walked to the edge of the woods, into the privacy of the shadows. Hamish unbuttoned her coat and explored beneath her cardigan, finding the zip of her heavy, wool dress. He slid his hands inside, resting on the curve of her lower back.

Ophelia was helpless to resist, melting into his green-flecked eyes, framed in lashes the same darkly ginger hue as his wild, curling hair. He raised her slightly in his arms, his beard against her cheek, his lips soft, yet kissing her with increasing ardour. Submerged within those kisses, and the dark cloth of early evening, Ophelia felt no hesitation, only the yearning to be loved and to give her own passion in return.

SOMETHING IN THE SHADOWS

DECEMBER 12TH, 1928

'HURRY UP!' said Gladys, skirting around the wall of the vegetable garden. 'I've only got half an hour before Cook'll be looking for me.'

'Right you are, lassie,' said Murray. 'Keep going, as far as the trees. No one'll bother us in there.'

'Oooh,' gasped Gladys, once they'd found a private spot, behind a large oak. 'You're awful good with your hands, even if they do smell of Chapman's horse liniment.'

'Just tell me which bits you want rubbing, Gladys, and I'll have you whickering like the fillies in the stables before feeding time.'

'What sort of girl do you think I am?' admonished Gladys. However, she wasted no time in grasping his behind.

'You're a woman, Gladys,' replied Murray, giving her ear a nibble. 'A woman who knows what she wants.'

'You're right there,' said Gladys. 'I've no time for being coy.' Her fingers found the bulge in Murray's trousers. 'Just make sure you control yourself at the end. I don't want to be getting a bun in the oven.'

'Oh, Gladys,' murmured Murray. 'Say the word and I'll put the ring on your finger. I'll be head groom one day, and we can have our own little cottage on the estate. With your hips, we'll have a family of eight before you can say pease pudding.'

Gladys smiled. It was a nice enough thought, and she might say yes, one of these days.

It was a few minutes later, as Gladys was pulling on her under-drawers, that she heard the rustle in the bushes.

'Murray!' she hissed. 'It's a Peeping Tom. Someone's watching us.'

'Never! Bloody pervert!' Murray hoiked up his trousers, peering into the gloom. 'I can't see anyone, Gladys. Are you sure?'

'I heard him! Look, over there: a flash of something behind those trees, towards the lake.'

'I can't see nothing.' Murray stepped forward, looking to all sides. 'Do you want me to go find the blighter and give him what for?'

'No. Leave it be. It's too dark to be running about,' said Gladys, shaking down her skirts. 'Just don't ask me to come down here no more.'

BOTTOMLESS DEEPS

9AM, DECEMBER 23RD, 1928

'No time for dilly-dallying,' declared Mrs Beesby. 'We've more Christmas fancies to bake, as well as turnips, carrots, potatoes and parsnips to peel, thirty hares that need skinning, and eight geese to pluck. Sir Hector's deer has been hanging for a few days, so Mr Hamish is looking after that. He'll bring in the joints of meat later, and we can tie them for roasting.'

The cook went to the knife drawer and pulled out a selection for sharpening.

'Our Ethel's complaining of a fever. I've telephoned for the doctor, and sent her back to bed, but I can't have anyone catching her ailment in the meantime, so leave her be. I'll take her some broth myself later on.'

Mrs Beesby turned to Hettie. 'We'll move you into one of the smaller rooms at the far end. There's some trunks in there, with odds and ends of storage, but I know you won't mind.

'I beg your pardon, Mrs Beesby,' said the butler, who had just popped his head into the kitchen. 'Sir Hector has bagged ten brace of pheasant this morning. The men have them on the cart outside.'

'Thank you, Mr Haddock,' said the cook. 'We certainly won't be short for feeding our guests. We've the Colonel and Miss Ellingmore arriving this afternoon, with her sister, not to mention all the others on Christmas Eve and the morning of the wedding.'

'No rest for the wicked,' grumbled Gertie, though loud enough that only Gladys might hear.

'Before I forget, Hettie, you'll be busy with the linens. You might ask Gertie and Gladys to help you make up the beds. There won't be a room empty by the time everyone's turned up. No more washing-up for you. We've young Susan to take charge of the sink now,' said Mrs Beesby.

Susan, slight and pale, and already up to her elbows in suds, looked over her shoulder and nodded her head at Hettie.

'Not much of a promotion if you ask me,' sniffed Bessie. 'I'd take greasy pots over soiled bedsheets any day. I wouldn't touch Sir Hector's without a pair of long-handled tongs.'

'I heard that, Bessie,' reprimanded the cook. 'Keep those sorts of thoughts to yourself, if you please. A change is as good as a rest.' She turned to Hettie.

'You keep your head down and work hard, Hettie. You're a good girl.' She gave her an encouraging pat on the shoulder.

The cook took off her apron and wrapped her shawl around her shoulders. 'Now, I'm going out to see to the pheasants. Make a start on those vegetables, girls.'

'Too good by all accounts,' whispered Gertie, giving Bessie a nudge. 'You know she was stepping out with Murray, from the stables? Well, it's all gone to the wind. I heard he tried it on fresh and she told him what for. All very respectable but you can't expect to tether a man without giving him a few oats to munch on.'

Bessie reached for a carrot.

'He's free again, is he? Winter's a long season without anyone to cuddle. If he wants to rummage under my skirts, I won't be saying 'no'!'

'Join the queue, Bessie,' winked Gladys. 'We were having a canoodle last night and I managed a fair assessment of his tackle. I've no complaints!'

'Saucy mare!' cackled Gertie, attacking her parsnip with renewed vigour.

'Mind you, I won't be going in those woods again,' added Gladys. 'Someone was there, I'm sure of it.'

'What! Watching you, like?'

Gertie and Bessie looked up from the pile of root vegetables.

'That's what I think.' Gladys dropped her voice. 'Murray says it might've been a spirit or some such. He's more superstitious than me. Believes in all sorts.'

'That's stable folk for you,' said Gertie. 'They've more charms and talismans and what not than you can fathom. No green near the horses and only plaiting their manes to an even number. All sorts of nonsense.'

Gladys tapped a carrot against her teeth in contemplation. 'He dreamt about a black horse, he says, before we had news of the Colonel and Miss Ellingmore, and everyone knows that seeing dark horses in your dreams foretells a wedding.'

'Perhaps there's something in it,' added Bessie. Cook says some parts of the loch are bottomless. Who knows what's lurking? Might have been some kelpie or pixie or summat.'

'It wasn't no kelpie,' said Gladys. 'They're supposed to lure you into water, and we weren't nowhere near the loch. Only went as far as the edge of the woods, as we didn't have much time.' She bit the top off the carrot. 'Mind you, they didn't hang about long. I heard a rustle in the bushes, and then saw something moving further off, towards the water. Murray would've followed whoever it was, if I'd let him.'

'There we are then,' said Bessie. 'Could've been a kelpie.'

'Or a ghost,' chimed in Susan, turning from the sink. 'My mam told me that Castle Kintochlochie is haunted. All those fine ladies made to marry old men they didn't like and throwing themselves out of the windows, and poor housemaids swimming out to drown in the loch because the laird had got them up the duff. Place is probably teeming with them. My mam's said I've got to keep my door locked and not peep outside, no matter what I hear.'

'It's wise advice to keep your door locked,' sniggered Gertie, 'But not against ghosts. More like, you'll find that cheeky wotsit McFinn, the footman, come to climb in bed with you.'

Susan frowned. 'She didn't say nothing about that. Only the ghosts.'

'All I know,' said Gladys, 'Is that summat was out there that shouldna been: be it ghost, or kelpie or some dirty bugger.'

NEVER TOO OLD FOR LOVE

2PM, DECEMBER 23RD, 1928

HADDOCK HAD JUST POURED Morag and Constance a cup of tea when McFinn entered to let her Ladyship know that the Colonel's Daimler was approaching.

The Colonel's Labrador, Rex, was the first to bound from the motor, his nose taking him straight to the lawns and the smell of rabbits. He was followed by a woman with salt and peppered hair, cut in an indeterminate style, wearing a man's tweed coat and walking boots. 'I'll go with Rexy down to the lake,' she called over her shoulder. 'I'll join you in a jiffy.'

'Right-oh, Marjorie,' said Enid. 'Come on, Monty. Let's get out of the cold. My toes are frozen!'

'Darlings!' cried Morag, greeting them as they came through the door. 'How was the journey? Were there flurries of snow higher up?' She kissed her old friends warmly.

'What ho, Morag!' bellowed the Colonel. 'I've come good at last, haven't I, bagging such a gorgeous bride?'

'I want to hear all your news!' laughed Morag. Including the details of your proposal. I hope you managed on one knee, Monty!'

'We've had the most marvellous time!' Enid squeezed her friend's hand. 'Marjorie's with us. She's just taken Rex for a quick walk.'

'We've so missed you,' said Morag, taking Enid's arm. 'I've put you and Monty in adjoining rooms, and Marjorie a little further down the corridor. McFinn will bring in your bags. I know you must be dying to freshen up, but do come and have a cup of tea first.'

'How beautiful everything looks,' said Enid, gazing up at the enormous Christmas tree, filling the double-height hallway almost to the upper ceiling.

'Doesn't it,' agreed Morag. 'Hamish and his men hauled it into place last week. Ophelia spent three days decorating. She has a marvellous head for heights, whizzing up the ladder like an acrobat.'

'We're going to have the loveliest Christmas! Almost like those when Hugo and Teddy were with us.' Morag gave a sniff and whipped a handkerchief from her pocket. 'Ignore me! I'm so happy for you both, and so delighted that we're celebrating your wedding here.'

'Now, do come through to the drawing room. Constance and Ophelia are eager to see you, and Horatio. You remember Mr Buffington? His extra-ordinary portrait of me remains much admired. He arrived yesterday, with his photographic apparatus, and has promised to take some lovely shots of you both, and the wedding party. We'll frame the best, so you can hang it in your new home.'

'What a clever present,' said Enid, giving her old friend a kiss upon the cheek. 'Do lead on, Morag dear. My feet are positively ice-bound.'

The fire was blazing merrily as Constance, Ophelia and Horatio rose from their seats to offer their own kisses of welcome. The huge hearth, garlanded in holly, brightly berried, occupied a good portion of the wall. Mistletoe hung from the chandelier and, with the light already fading, candles had been lit, giving the room a cosy feel. Pudding lay on a rug, toasting herself comfortably, in the company of Braveheart, Hamish's loyal wolfhound, and the beady-eyed Aphrodite.

'Daphne, my daughter, and her husband Peter, arrived this morning, but she's resting, I'm afraid,' said Morag, urging the Colonel into an armchair and passing a platter of teacakes, hot and buttery. 'Peter's already with Hector somewhere: fishing, or shooting something. They'll be with us for dinner, of course, as will Hamish. He's gone to check on the horses.'

'I haven't seen Daphne since she was in pigtails,' mused Enid, accepting a cup of steaming tea and settling onto the sofa beside her old friend. 'Always such a polite girl.'

Constance laughed. 'She's changed a little since then. Very much the elegant hostess.'

'You must try some of Mrs Beesby's Christmas cake, Colonel,' said Ophelia, 'I helped stir the charms in.'

'Thank you, my dear.' He leaned in close. 'Put a drop of whisky in this tea for me, will you? The pipes need some lubrication.'

'So, Ophelia,' began Enid. 'Have you been turning Castle Kintochlochie on its head? All the local young men must be in love with you.'

'There are surprisingly few suitors in these parts, Enid, but now that my mother's here, I'm sure she'll rectify that. She'll be whisking me off to Balmoral to lasso some minor royal. No one will be safe.'

'Ludicrous girl,' said Enid, giving Ophelia's cheek a pinch. 'Unless your eyes have been quite closed, I'm sure you've noticed a very eligible man right under your nose. Morag wrote to tell me that he'd returned from Edinburgh.'

'What's that?' brayed the Colonel. 'Is there another wedding on the cards? Stealing our thunder, what!'

'Not at all.' Ophelia bit into a mince pie, brimming with hot sultanas, and sugary on top. 'I'm in no hurry on that account.'

'Might we have more tea, Haddock,' said Morag, turning to the butler, who stood quietly to one side. 'And then sherries all round. I'm sure we'll be ready for them.'

'I'd like to hear about your trip to the Lake District,' said Ophelia mischievously. 'Did you have fun practising at being Mrs Faversham?'

'Really, Ophelia!' reprimanded Lady Morag. 'Too, too naughty of you!'

'It's quite alright.' Enid smiled. 'I did, and it certainly did feel illicit, although I don't think we were the only ones signing ourselves in under slightly false pretences.' She popped a slice of shortbread onto her plate. 'We stayed in the quaintest of hotels, stuffed with octogenarians. More old survivors than bright young things but what dreadful fun we all had! Don't let anyone tell you that there's no reheating old cabbage.'

'You've never been cabbage, my dearest.' Morag chuckled. 'And there's nothing old about you!'

The Colonel reached over to give Enid's leg a squeeze. 'What's my lovely bride-to-be saying, hmm… telling you all our exploits? I must say it's done me the power of good. I feel a new man.'

'And what have you been writing, Enid?' asked Constance, tactfully changing the direction of the conversation. 'I know you're always penning something exciting.'

'I've just finished my latest novel.' Enid beamed. 'It may be my most sensational yet. It's all about the amorous adventures of a French courtesan. She beds one dashing suitor after another, moving on as soon as she's bored, claiming ever greater conquests. It's sure to be a bestseller.'

'Hmm…' said Horatio, leaning to whisper in Ophelia's ear. 'I wonder who provided the inspiration for that…?'

The door pushed open and Rex came lumbering in, flopping down to join the canine assembly before the fire. He was closely followed by a woman of middle-age, wearing flannel trousers and a Fair Isle patterned jumper.

'Hello everyone, sorry to be late to the party. I'm Marjorie, Enid's sister. Lovely of you to invite me.'

'Oh!' exclaimed Morag, surprised at the firmness of Marjorie's handshake. 'It's our pleasure.'

'I'm jolly pleased to meet you. Enid tells me that you're all a solid bunch.' Marjorie took a seat beside Ophelia. 'I see you keep several of the rarer sheep breeds, as well as your Highland cows. They look fine specimens,' said Marjorie, enthusiastically filling her plate with sandwiches. 'Perhaps you'll fill me in on what sort of fodder you're giving them. I met a handsome fellow near the stables and he told me you've been employing some new methods, to ensure the comfort of your livestock. Anything that improves animal welfare is worth our support, I say.'

Marjorie paused to take a gulp of tea.

'I work for the Royal Society for the Prevention of Cruelty to Animals, at the headquarters in Jermyn Street. I must say that it's good to be out of London and in the countryside. I do miss the fresh air; so restorative.'

'How fascinating,' remarked Ophelia. 'Although I expect you have some rather sad stories to tell. So many don't understand the responsibility of caring for another living creature, and it breaks my heart to think of all the pets who think they've arrived in a loving home, only to be turfed out with the tinsel in the new year.'

'Quite!' Marjorie selected a slice of Dundee cake. 'But we're doing our best to educate people. We've the support of some well-known figures too. Rudyard Kipling is lobbying for free veterinary centres for animals in India, and that marvellous actor, Gerald du Maurier, is on our side too.'

'Goodness me, Marjorie, you're moving in exciting circles these days,' said Enid. 'I'd no idea.'

'I met his daughter, Daphne, at a party once,' recalled Ophelia. 'She's terribly clever. She told me she was planning a novel: some family saga set in Cornwall. Starts and ends with a wedding, I think.'

'That's Daphne alright,' said Marjorie. 'She's a curious girl. Showed me one of her short stories. Not at all like your romantic gushings, Enid. Much darker. I've promised to purchase a copy when she makes it into print.'

'Well, there are enough readers for us all,' answered Enid, gratefully accepting a sherry from the tray proffered by Haddock. 'Wouldn't it be dull if we all wrote the same thing?'

'Hear, hear,' said Morag, raising her glass. 'A toast to following what brings us joy, in whatever form it presents itself.'

Haddock surveyed the sherry bottle. He could see that another trip to the cellar would be necessary.

'Oooh!' cried Ophelia, looking to the window. 'It's started snowing!'

'So it has.' Morag frowned. 'Oh, I do hope it doesn't prevent our guests from arriving. Most are driving over tomorrow and on Christmas morning itself. The mountain pass becomes perilous once it's icy.'

Ophelia patted the window seat, beckoning Horatio to sit beside her.

'I've been wanting to have a private conversation with you all day,' she chided. 'Where did you get to?'

'Setting up a dark room, darling, for developing my photographs. Cecil has been a dear, showing me how things are done. I don't aspire to create the masterpieces Mr Beaton conjures from simple flesh, but I'll do my best for lovely Enid. Every bride should have some photographs from which to remember her happy day.'

Horatio lowered his voice to a conspiratorial whisper. 'Even if she is sentenced to spend the rest of her life with someone as awful as the Colonel.'

'Now, now!' chided Ophelia. 'He's much improved since we last met him. Enid seems to have been a civilizing influence.'

Horatio rolled his eyes. 'If you say so, my dearest.'

'Do tell me more about Paris?'

'Utterly divine, as ever. I've been creating a series of male nudes. The photography is marvellously handy, darling. I'll be painting on canvas eventually, but will use the shots as *aide-memoires*. So much easier to find willing models on the Continent. You've no idea how many young men were willing to show their all... in the name of art, of course.'

'Naturally,' said Ophelia, smiling widely.

'Mmmn... I made a thoroughly hands-on study of some of my subjects.'

'Really Horatio, you are too, too dreadful!'

'Ah...there's only one man to whom I'd vow eternal faithfulness, besides the one you've bagged, Ophelia.' Horatio drew a heart onto the steamed window pane. 'But you're yet to set the date... are your feet cold? Perhaps there's someone else who's taken your fancy?'

'Hardly! Most of the men who come calling here only have half their teeth while the rest have a double-portion of everything.'

Horatio raised an eyebrow. 'Everything?'

'I'm talking about abundance of waistline.' Ophelia gave Horatio a reprimanding elbow in the ribs.

'Now, my dear, speaking as an artist, I must congratulate you on the festive décor. You've transformed this place beautifully. The silver bells and stars hanging from the ballroom chandeliers are positively genius, and I've never seen so much mistletoe. You have flair! You have style! You are a goddess!'

'I know,' Ophelia replied modestly.

DELICIOUS DELIGHTS

5.30PM, DECEMBER 23RD, 1928

OPHELIA STRETCHED LANGUOROUSLY, enjoying the sensation of cotton sheets upon her bare skin.

'The wallpaper in here is so dark. It's nowhere near as nice as mine.'

Smiling, she watched Hamish walk over to pour them both a glass of water. How muscular Hamish's back was, and all the rest of him. There was something to be said for a man who wielded an axe on a regular basis and could haul fifty sheep through a trough of dip in less than an hour.

'I hope Mummy appreciates my having swapped rooms with her. Only right I suppose, seeing as mine's on the corner, and has absolutely the best views. She and Daddy don't usually share a bedroom in London, but they are here. Perhaps it'll put her in a better mood and she'll stop nagging me about finding a suitable husband.'

'Lady Daphne is charming, and I'm sure has your best interests at heart,' said Hamish.

'You only think that because you don't know her,' retorted Ophelia. 'Besides which, she'd be rather less charming if she knew you were having your wicked way with me.'

She wiggled her toes contentedly.

'It was very kind of you to collect her and daddy from the station, but even having changed into your best tweeds to do so won't stop her from thinking of you as 'one of the staff'. She's a frightful snob, and won't be happy unless she bags me an earl, at the very least.'

She propped herself up on one elbow, taking in the tightness of Hamish's buttocks, and the fullness of what lay between his legs, still standing at moderate attention after their recent tumble.

He gave her a half-smile as he pulled on his shirt. Isn't that exactly what you thought of me the day you first arrived, little London Miss?'

'You have me there...' admitted Ophelia, a slight blush rising to her cheek. She changed the subject swiftly. 'The Willow Pattern room is pretty, but doesn't get enough sun, being north facing. Far too cold! Of course, it does have the advantage of being nearly opposite yours, with only the bathroom and the linen cupboards at this end of the corridor. More convenient than my old room!'

She watched as Hamish fastened his buttons. 'It'll be me doing the sneaking in the middle of the night now. No more waiting for you to make your entrance. You'd better be ready for me, when-ever I choose to slip through your door.'

Ophelia gave him a saucy smile and allowed the coverlet to slip.

'I'm at your command,' answered Hamish, giving her a mock bow, and looking appreciatively as Ophelia sat up, allowing him a better view of her own delightful curves. 'Now, help me find my cufflinks, won't you? I seem to be mislaying all sorts of things lately.'

'All that you need is right here,' replied Ophelia, pushing the quilt away altogether, and parting her legs for him. 'I'm certain you'll stop thinking about your cufflinks if you only come and give me a kiss.'

'I'll take a pre-dinner aperitif,' said Hamish, climbing back onto the bed. 'I'm quite thirsty, so you'd better lie still until I've drunk my fill.'

His hands lifted her hips, bringing the sweet centre of her to his mouth, his beard pleasurably rough against the tender skin of her inner thighs.

'Oh yes,' sighed Ophelia. 'Take what you like, my darling.'

Pudding, having been waiting long enough, in her eyes, decided that her patience was spent. With an imperious 'arooo', she bounded onto the quilt, sticking her cold nose in the vicinity of a certain taut behind.

'Don't be cross with her,' laughed Ophelia, seeing the expression on Hamish's face. 'She only wants to join in the fun!'

THE SECRET TO A HAPPY MARRIAGE

COCKTAIL HOUR, 7PM, DECEMBER 23RD, 1928

GIGGLING, Ophelia scampered ahead of Hamish, down to the main hall. They inspected one another's appearance at the foot of the stairs, Ophelia brushing some fluff from the shoulder of Hamish's kilt jacket, while he passed his hands down her body, squeezing the curve of her bottom beneath her velvet evening gown. They exchanged a lingering kiss.

'If I wasn't so hungry, I'd take you straight back to bed,' murmured Hamish, adjusting the sporran hanging to the front of his kilt.

Ophelia pulled him close. 'Let's hope Mrs Beesby sends out the courses quickly. I'll feign a headache once we've been served the main course, and you can pretend you need to check on Esmeralda. Isn't she due to foal?'

Hamish nuzzled her ear. 'I don't usually commend the telling of untruths, but let's make an exception...'

'It's all in a good cause.' Ophelia smiled. 'You're so much more appreciative of my company than my mother. It is lovely that she's travelled up to see me, and daddy too, but she has plans for me that are far more in her interest than mine.'

'Giddy up then,' said Hamish. 'The sooner we get the nosebags on, the sooner I'll have you back upstairs and out of this delightful dress.'

~

In the drawing room, Hector was already well-lubricated, holding forth to Sir Peter and the Colonel on the day's shooting. 'Damn fine day on the moor. You're not bad with your gun, Peter, I must say.' Hector grinned widely, showing a mouthful of yellowed teeth. 'It's open season on rabbit and pigeon all year round, of course, but we only have a few more weeks for most of the other birds. Mustn't waste any opportunity.'

Colonel Faversham raised his glass to Hector and Sir Peter. 'Sorry to have missed it, old chap. Still, I'll be out with the guns next time I visit. I'll catch up then.'

'Ha! We'll see about that. I don't plan on being out-performed by a fellow with only one eye,' declared Hector, taking a hefty swig of whisky.

The Colonel glared at Hector with his one good orb, before Sir Peter decided to change the tangent of conversation.

'Mildred Faucett-Plumbly would probably out-bag us all.' Sir Peter smiled wryly. '*The Field* has named her as one of the best shots of the year again, and well-deserved, so I hear.'

'It's been a particularly good season for goose,' went on Hector. 'We've plenty for the wedding celebrations. That and partridge.'

Enid hurried over. 'Do change the subject, darlings. Marjorie will be down in a minute and while she acknowledges the traditions of country life, she's dreadfully against blood sports. I can't say that I blame her: all those horrid explosions and birds dropping out of the sky.'

'Quite!' added Ophelia, overhearing from her position on the sofa, seated next to her mother. 'I'm not at all keen myself, and neither is Hamish, if you must know. No one who loves animals can take pleasure in such pursuits, even where some culling is necessary.'

'Really, Ophelia,' said Lady Daphne, looking up from her martini with a disapproving frown. 'I'm sure I didn't raise you to express your opinions so forcefully, or in such a tone. A young lady should know when to keep quiet.'

Ophelia felt her temperature rising but contented herself with turning her back and sticking her tongue out at Horatio, who was seated by the window, wearing an amused expression.

'You won't be complaining when it's on your plate, what!' barked Hector. 'Venison, too. I bagged a beautiful hind the other day. Saw the stag but had to leave it: no stalking those until July comes around again. Dashed shame, but there you go. Rules are there for a reason.'

'What's on the menu, tonight,' asked the Colonel. 'Do we know?'

'Trout pâté, followed by lamb, I think, and beef consommé to start,' said Constance, accepting her customary sherry from Haddock.

'Damn good cook you have here, Morag. Food always toothsome and she doesn't stinge on the helpings.' The Colonel looked pointedly at his watch. 'Where's Marjorie gotten to? I'm hungry enough to eat a horse.'

'I'm here,' came a voice from the doorway.

Marjorie strode over to sit beside Enid, leaning in to speak in a hushed tone. 'Sorry to be late. I've put on a few pounds since I last wore this dress and the hooks were a trifle tricky.'

'You look lovely,' said Enid, giving her sister a kiss on the cheek. 'You've time for an aperitif before we go in.' She nodded fondly at her husband. 'Ignore Monty; he's always ravenous.'

'I'll just have a quick one, Monty. Don't worry. I'm pretty peckish myself.' Marjorie took a glass and knocked her sherry back in one swipe.

'Bravo, old girl, that's the ticket.' The Colonel clapped his hands together and eyed their hostess. 'Morag, let's proceed, shall we? May I have the honour?' With that, he led her by the arm, dining-room bound.

~

Ophelia managed to claim a seat between Hamish and Horatio, and found herself rather enjoying her meal. Mrs Beesby was a superb cook, and Ophelia's afternoon frolics had left her famished. Everyone seemed to eat quickly, working their way through the courses with relish.

Lady Daphne was discussing Paris fashions, having just returned from another trip. Horatio voiced his admiration of her gown: an enchanting design, in raspberry red velvet, with full rose blossoms sewn from the shoulder diagonally through the bodice, to the hem.

Ophelia had to admit that it suited her mother perfectly. Another trip to Antoine's in Paris had ensured that her bob remained as sleek as ever. Her hair, a lustrous shade of dark brown, was like Ophelia's own, but without the maddening curls Ophelia was obliged to tame.

'It's from Lucien Lelong,' said Lady Daphne. 'The longer length skirt is most practical for Scotland. One hardly needs worry about the cold. Impossible to heat these rooms, and I do so dislike being chilly.'

'Oh, Lady Daphne!' cooed Horatio. 'I can see you with a plunging décolleté. Only the most elegant of women can carry off such elements without appearing vulgar.'

'How kind of you to say so. Although I always believe that clothes shouldn't be too conspicuous. Chanel's Ford dress is a staple in my wardrobe.'

Beneath the table, Ophelia gave Horatio's shin a poke with her toe. He was such a flatterer! Besides which, she couldn't help feeling envious. Her mother had quite enough male attention without stealing Horatio's as well.

'I do adore Lelong's designs,' continued Horatio, giving Ophelia's elbow a returning pinch. 'Those darling crepes and chiffons in pastel shades, transformed for evening when worn with a diamond-embroidered fichu. So terribly clever if one is travelling light.'

'And his fragrances,' sighed Daphne. 'Such mystery! Such romance! And the bottles so incredibly pretty! I'm not in the least surprised that Princess Nathalie agreed to marry him last year.'

'But, you know,' said Horatio, leaning a little closer to Daphne's ear, 'The marriage is a sham! Ethereal and glamorous as Nathalie is, Lucien is in love with one of his models, and Nathalie has been seen with that delicious young dancer, Serge Lifar. French-Ukrainian you know, and swoon-making in his ballet tights! All deadly scandalous!'

'Ah,' sighed Lady Daphne. 'But one can forgive them anything. His craftsmanship is beyond compare, as is her exquisite taste.'

Ophelia stabbed an asparagus tip in annoyance. Really! Her mother could be such a hypocrite! She turned to the conversation on her other side, where Hamish was discussing politics with her father.

'Dreadful what's happening in Italy.' Sir Peter shook his head. 'The Grand Council of Fascism now has the right to approve the succession to the throne, as well as the monarch's powers. Poor King Victor Emmanuel has opposed it of course, but he can do little except grumble.'

'I applaud the spirit behind such reforms,' admitted Hamish, slicing into his lamb. 'But not the manner of their implementation.

Estates are being forced to cultivate extensively, to help feed the populace, but it seems wrong to dispossess the aristocracy for failing to comply effectively.'

'It'll be the firing squads next,' Sir Peter agreed, chewing thoughtfully on a roast potato. 'Can't help but think of the fate of the Imperial royal family...'

'Of course, I'm all for workers receiving a fair wage. Too many landowners have had things their own way for far too long.' Hamish turned to Ophelia. 'We've been working to renovate some of the estate cottages, Ophelia and I, and to give our men a vested interest in the forestry side of things. We're agreeing to share ten percent of the income with all the workers, to encourage them in their labours.'

Ophelia gave Hamish a complicit smile.

'That's pretty progressive.' Sir Peter nodded. 'Perhaps I'll try something similar on the Norfolk turkey farm. It's doing rather well, and it's only right, as you say, to properly reward men for their work.'

Ophelia loved hearing Hamish speak about things that mattered. When it came to his workers, he was passionately committed to protecting their health and welfare.

Feeling more benevolent, she turned once more to her left.

'You should hear my husband speak in Parliament some time,' Lady Daphne was telling Horatio. 'He's splendidly modest, but he's a rising star in the Conservative party. I've no doubt the Prime Minister will offer him a Cabinet position before long.'

How funny, Ophelia thought to herself, I'd not realized it before, but mother admires my father in the same way that I do Hamish. Perhaps that's the answer to a happy marriage. Not just love, and enjoying how they make you feel, but having respect for their principles.

It was only as she scraped round for the last spoonful of apple dumpling and custard that she remembered her intention of feigning a migraine. Hamish was still chatting animatedly to her father. She decided not to interrupt them. They had the rest of their lives, after all, to make love...

THE NEED FOR AN HEIR

ALMOST MIDNIGHT, 23RD DECEMBER, 1928

Adjusting the abundant pillows behind her on the bed, Lady Daphne sighed. 'I don't know what my mother is thinking. I hear she's had papers drawn up to leave the castle and estate in Ophelia's guardianship until a son is produced. Thankfully, the conditions of the earldom allow the title to skip several generations.' She reached for the pot of beeswax cream on the nightstand and rubbed it into her fingernails. 'So unfortunate that neither Mama nor I have been blessed with boys, but Ophelia may yet produce a male heir, if we can only find her a suitable husband.'

Sir Peter poured cocoa into his wife's cup and passed it to her before climbing into bed himself.

'A good job, my dear, that your father was the only son among seven girls, or the estate, and title, might have passed to some brotherly sibling when he died. I shall never get the hang of these laws of inheritance among the aristocracy. They defy all reason.'

'Quite so. One might almost think this family cursed. My father's own father had but one brother himself and, as you know, he died before being able to sire issue.'

'Hardly cursed, my love,' reproached her husband. 'We're very happy aren't we, and Ophelia is a joy to us both.'

Lady Daphne waved her hand airily. 'Yes, yes... but you know what I mean, Peter. We can't just look to ourselves. We must think of the future.'

He dropped a kiss upon his wife's shoulder. 'I believe I can foresee how the next half an hour might unfold, if you finish up that cocoa, my darling.'

'You're insatiable, Peter!' she admonished, though placing her cup swiftly upon the bedside and extinguishing the light. 'Once a day ought to be enough for anyone!'

'Not if they're married to the most seductive woman in all the British Isles,' he countered, untying the ribbon at the top of her nightgown and burying his head in her breast.

'Goodness me!' sighed Daphne, as her husband's hand travelled up her thigh, to cup the underside of her bottom.

Not for the first time, Lady Daphne Finchingfield was reminded that she had not married Sir Peter purely for his wealth, or the prestige of his career. He was handsome, strong and highly principled, and he positively adored her. *With my body, I thee worship* was a dictate he followed on a daily basis.

Opening herself to the dominance of his embrace, she felt the familiar shiver of pleasure.

~

It was barely ten minutes later that Lady Daphne realized they were not alone. An apparition, as she explained later, had been standing at the foot of the bed, dressed all in white, pale, and bearing an expression of malicious intent. Sir Peter, buried beneath the covers at that moment, ensuring his wife reached a peak of transcendent delight to match his own, had his doubts.

Daphne wasn't one to spout rubbish about spectral forms, and she had no time for the séances that continued to be fashionable among her set, but she had been known to lose her head in the throes of passion. Hadn't she fainted just the other week, Sir Peter reminded himself, during a particularly satisfying bout of love-making? She'd told him that she'd seen such a blinding light that she'd imagined herself passed to the next plane.

Dashed shaming, having all and sundry knocking on the door, alarmed by Daphne's screams. As if I'd been murdering her!

The phantasm had disappeared as quickly as it had risen, but had left a sense of the horrors in its wake. Even with the door firmly bolted and the lamp left burning, Daphne had refused his further attentions.

SPECULATION

MORNING, CHRISTMAS EVE, 1928

'DID you ever hear the like of it!' said Gertie, setting the cloths on the morning tea trays. 'Screaming blue murder and waking everyone from their beds. The Colonel came out with his revolver, apparently.'

'Didn't wake me up,' said McFinn, lounging against the table. 'I was having a very tasty dream about her n'all. Nice-looking bit of skirt, that Lady Daphne.'

'Don't let Mrs Beesby hear you talking that way,' snapped Gertie. 'You'll be out on yer ear, and we're short-handed enough as it is.'

'It's the kelpie,' said Bessie. 'Driven in by the snow. Wasn't it all in white?' She reached the marmalade down from the shelf. 'Kelpies sometimes appear as white horses, you know, shaking their manes as they beckon you to your death.'

'It wasn't no horse, you ninny,' scoffed McFinn. 'It were wearing a white cape, she said, with a hood. Terrifying, apparently.'

He pinched a hot biscuit from the griddle, blowing on it before popping it into his mouth.

'I didn't know they were even in that room,' moaned Gladys, pouring water into each teapot. 'No one tells me nothing round here. I'd have waltzed in with the morning tray thinking it was Lady Ophelia in bed, and found her parents instead. Bloomin' embarrassing.'

'My money's on a ghost,' said McFinn, dropping crumbs onto one of the trays.

'My mam said...' began Susan.

'Yes, we know,' sighed Gertie, brushing away the offensive crumbs and glaring at McFinn. 'The castle is brimming with ghosts: the ancient ladies of Kintochlochie, doomed to roam the castle after killing themselves... She may be right, but I've never seen one.'

'I heard footsteps last night,' added Susan. 'I pulled the covers over my eyes and said the Lord's Prayer three times to keep me safe.'

'Didn't Mary tell us something about that corridor on the second floor?' added Gertie. 'Secret passages used by the fine ladies to rendezvous with their lovers? She hears all the interesting stuff, being up with Lady Morag.'

'What's this?' said Mrs Beesby, bustling into the kitchen. 'I go into the pantry for five minutes and there's lewd talk! Gertie, you should be setting an example to Susan, not fuelling her imagination.'

Carrying a basket of dirty clothes, Hettie tottered into the kitchen.

'Ah, Hettie, there you are,' added the cook. 'You've Mr Hamish's shirts I see. Make sure you give them a good scrubbing. He's out with the men all hours of the day, and his clothes show the evidence. Give the collars a good once over. Do you want a hand in pressing them after? You might show Susan how to use the iron.'

'No thank you, Mrs Beesby.' Hettie clutched the shirts tight.

'No one can do them like me. I'll make them like new, even if my fingers are rubbed raw.'

'Well, that's a commendable attitude.' Mrs Beesby smiled. 'But no need to overdo it. Your mother was a hard worker too, I remember, back when she worked here. Like Susan's grandmother. They'd be proud of you both, I'm sure.'

'Now, let's get those trays sorted, and we'll start on breakfast proper,' said Mrs Beesby. 'Then it's all hands on deck for making pies and pastries and the usual festive titbits. The hordes will be descending and they'll be wanting to be fed in a grand manner. It might be Christmas upstairs but there won't be any time for festivities down here until we've prepared the banquets they'll be expecting.'

FRENCH FANCIES

2PM, CHRISTMAS EVE, 1928

OPHELIA SAT in the window-seat of the drawing room, her legs tucked under, stroking the length of Pudding's back. With a sigh, she looked out at the landscape of wild crags, dappled white, rising from beyond the frosted loch. Pudding, too, peered wistfully through the window.

'Such a bore having to sit inside, waiting to spring into action as the welcoming hostess,' she grumbled.

Horatio looked up from his book. 'We might put the radio on, dearest, or the gramophone. Jolly us up a little.'

'It is awfully quiet,' admitted Marjorie, her knitting needles pausing in the creation of something in a muddy shade of green. 'If we had a fourth, we could play bridge. Is Constance about?'

'Having some hems taken up,' replied Ophelia. 'Enid and the Colonel are lying down, and Granny said she needed to check menus with Mrs Beesby.'

Horatio plucked at the dog-hairs littering the sofa. 'I saw

Hector, earlier; asked if I wanted to watch him clean his shotguns!'
He rolled his eyes heavenward. 'Really, my dears!'

'My, what an exciting offer! And you turned him down?'
Ophelia smirked.

Horatio threw a cushion across the room, which Ophelia
caught adeptly and tucked under her elbow.

'At least we're spared Felicité's company.' Ophelia opened
Morag's copy of The Lady, flicked through, and then cast it aside.
'She was supposed to arrive late last night, with this new husband
of hers, but they didn't show. With any luck, she's changed her
mind about coming.'

'I've no idea where Daddy's got to, except that he's bound to be
avoiding Hector, and Mummy's having a long soak in the bath.
She's still quite shaken by what she thinks she saw last night, and
insists the hot water will relax her.'

Pulling Pudding closer, Ophelia gave her a good scratch behind
the ears. 'Honestly, you'd think she'd be beyond imagining spectres
at the chime of midnight. She spent her childhood here, so she
knows the castle is full of strange noises and draughts that move
curtains.'

'She did give us rather a fright,' said Horatio. 'It took me an age
to get back to sleep.'

Marjorie set down her needles. 'We could go for a short walk.
Keep an eye on the road and trot back inside if we see a car
approaching. No one's expected for at least an hour yet.'

'Why not,' agreed Ophelia, already on her feet. 'Horatio, you'll
come out, won't you?'

'Of course, my dears. I've rather a hankering to make a
snowman and we might take the camera, to immortalize our
efforts.'

'What fun! I'll nip to the kitchen and ask Mrs Beesby for a few
carrots for their noses.'

The sky was a brilliant blue and the cold painfully crisp, though
exhilarating. Tiny diamonds of light sparkled through the snow,

thanks to the bright sunshine. There really was nowhere as beautiful, thought Ophelia, as the Kintochlochie valley and its mountains. Streaked white between darkly-jagged granite, these seemed to rise taller than ever. The castle looked almost like a giant's plaything beneath their towering splendour.

It was strangely quiet outside, the snow deadening all sounds. Their feet crunched through the new drifts but there was not a single bird to be heard, and the wind had dropped to nothing.

Pudding raced off, only her fluffy tail visible, making random trails through the fresh powder.

'It'll be a hard frost tonight, if the clouds don't come over,' remarked Marjorie. 'The shallows of the loch are freezing over, look. You might be able to skate by the new year.'

They were half-way through the third member of their snow family, Ophelia pushing a carrot into the face of their creation, when they heard Pudding bark, alerting them to a motor emerging from the mountain pass. It swung into view over the crest, then made its descent, down the steep hillside, before entering the first swathe of forest.

'Crikey!' Marjorie exclaimed. 'We'd better go in. You might want to dry your hair, Ophelia; Horatio landed a lucky shot with that snowball!'

'No time for all that,' declared Ophelia, breaking into a run. 'I'll just change my shoes. I'm not jumping through hoops for the Faucett-Plumbleys and the vicar, and all those old biddies. They won't care what I look like. They can take me, red nose and all.'

≈

Ophelia found Enid and the Colonel, alongside Morag and Constance, already seated in the drawing room, where the fire was blazing. Haddock had brought in afternoon tea, setting out the various plates of delicacies on the side cabinet: miniature sausage rolls, hot from the oven, the pastry light and flaky, and three types of cake, alongside an array of finger sandwiches. Horatio sidled over to sniff out those filled with smoked salmon.

'We've been watching you.' Enid smiled. 'You appeared to be having so much fun we didn't like to make you break off, but I see you spotted the car coming down.'

Ophelia gave the three ladies each a kiss upon the cheek.

'Will I do?' she asked, shaking her hair and shrugging off the thickest of her cardigans. She headed to the window before waiting for a reply, accepting a teacup from Haddock.

There was a crunch of wheels on gravel and Ophelia received a nudge from Horatio that sloshed a good amount of Darjeeling into her saucer. A slender woman stepped out, clad head to toe in silver fox, a curl of white-blonde hair slicking her cheek from beneath her fur hat. She paused momentarily to look into the car's wing mirror, applying another lashing of crimson lipstick, before sailing up to the front door.

Damn! thought Ophelia. She's arrived after all, and just when I'm looking a bit of a fright.

'Is that her husband?' Horatio craned his neck. 'Old enough to be her grandfather, but rich as Croesus, no doubt. You must warn her off, Ophelia dear, or she'll be dragging Hamish into service before the cucumber sandwiches are eaten. If that's what she's been bedding, she'll be slavering for firm flesh.'

'I trust Hamish completely,' hissed Ophelia. 'Besides which, I'm determined to be civil, no matter how poisonous she is.'

'You're far too saintly. If she were the former lover of my latest squeeze, I'd be readying a bottle of Dr. Caldwell's Colon-Purge.'

'I'm tempted, believe me,' admitted Ophelia. 'But Enid asked particularly for her to be invited, so my own dislike shall have to be put aside.'

There was a commotion in the hallway, and the door was flung open.

'At last, we are here,' announced Felicité, beaming a full-wattage smile at the assembled company. 'Such a journey *malheureux*! But now I am *avec mes vieilles copines*.'

She slithered out of her coat, which passed directly into Haddock's waiting arms, revealing a dress in the same shade of red as her lips.

'And we're delighted to welcome you, my dear,' said Morag, rising from her seat.

Felicité tossed her fox fur hat onto a chair, inspiring both Pudding and Aphrodite to make a beeline for the furry beast. Two fat little bottoms sat firmly upon its head, asserting their superiority over the interloper. Horatio and Ophelia exchanged a gleeful moment. Oblivious to the fate of her expensive *chapeau*, Felicité swept forward to offer her cheek to Morag.

'Such a happy occasion, and kind of you to make the trans-Atlantic journey,' said Morag.

'For Enid, how could I not!'

Felicité leaned to whisper in Morag's ear, though loud enough that Ophelia and Horatio, tucked in the window seat just behind, could overhear. 'Although I offer my commiseration on the groom being Colonel Faversham. I suppose, at a certain age, one must take what one can get.'

Horatio stifled a snigger, nudging Ophelia again. 'How marvellous. She's as foul as ever! Enid can only have asked her to come to provide fodder for her latest novel!'

'Besides which,' commented Ophelia, 'She's hardly one to talk. Her husband's at least thirty years older than the Colonel.'

'That may be part of the attraction, don't you think?' mused Horatio, hiding behind his teacup.

Felicité's next kisses were for the prospective bride. 'Congratulations, *ma chérie*. I see that you are radiant with happiness. The Colonel is fulfilling his duties, *n'est-ce pas*?'

Enid gave an indulgent laugh. 'We rub along very well. We're in the prime of life, and intend to make the most of all the years remaining to us.'

'Ah yes!' Felicité patted Enid's hand. 'Always a silver lining. The Colonel perhaps has only ten years in him, and then you shall be free again, *chère Enid.*'

Before Enid had the chance to reply, another figure entered the room, and conversation was brought to an astonished halt.

'Ah, my Wilberforce! Everyone, this is my new husband,' declared Felicité. 'We are the love-birds, married last week in Las Vegas.'

'That's right sweetie-pie, and you've made me the happiest of men.' He made his way to Felicité's side, a little unsteadily. 'What a pile! It's a swell old place you have here, Lady MacKintoch!'

'Mr Worthington, how lovely to meet you.' Morag made haste to hide her surprise at his aged years. 'And I must congratulate you on your acquisition of Lionheart Studios; I saw an article in *The Times*,' replied Morag. 'Of course, I've heard of your films, though I've not had the pleasure of seeing any. We're so remotely placed here, and I don't often get up to town.'

'You certainly are in the boondocks! We had a helluva drive getting here, and I've seen some roads in my time!'

'*Mon Dieu!* Wilberforce's tyre took a nail and we had to spend the night at the most unpleasant tavern,' chipped in Felicité, following Morag to the sofa and arranging her long legs to best advantage. 'Fortunately, a *charmant* young man came to our rescue: a Mr Belton? He was here for Morag's birthday party, *n'était-il pas?*'

'Of course,' said Lady Morag. 'Peregrine and his dear parents are invited to the nuptial celebrations. You were headed in the same direction I think, though the Beltons aren't due until the morning of the wedding. They have a lodge not far from here.'

'Wasn't he the one who took you for a drive?' whispered Horatio, giving Ophelia a wink.

'Shhh! I don't wish to be reminded!'

'Lady Morag,' said Felicité, speaking *sotto voce*, but knowing herself to be in earshot of the handsome McFinn, who stood behind with a tray of fondant fancies. 'May I request a separate bedroom for Wilberforce? He snores, and I must have my beauty sleep.'

She lowered her eyes. 'I find that once a week provides ample provision for his needs. The rest of the time, I like to ensure the bed is my own.'

'My dear, I understand completely,' said Lady Morag, though with an arch of her eyebrow.

'Ah, and who is this sitting so quietly in the corner,' declared Felicité, standing once more, and bearing down on Ophelia with arms outstretched, kissing the air a good two inches either side of her cheeks.

'But how tired you are looking, *ma chérie*,' said Felicité, her expression one of abject concern, 'And your nose such a colour! You're ailing, I think.'

She blew a kiss at Horatio, then glided onwards, resuming her seat upon the sofa.

'How does she manage it?' remarked Horatio. 'So effectively vile, in so economical an amount of words.'

Ophelia wriggled her toes in her wet stockings and scowled, wishing she had prepared herself more adequately for Felicite's scrutiny and her unique brand of disparagement.

'She's an utter, *utter* cow!'

ALL FUR COAT AND NO KNICKERS

6PM, CHRISTMAS EVE, 1928

'THAT FRENCH PIECE HAS SOME CHEEK,' said Gladys, licking the custard from her spoon and casting her eye down the kitchen table, where the staff were gathered for their evening meal.

'Coming back here after the carryings on last time. She's no shame, that woman. Leading Mr Hamish a merry dance, getting him to take her to the big city, and then dumping him when something better came along.'

'I've no complaints.' McFinn grinned. 'She was friendly enough with me.'

'We know how friendly she was with you!' retorted Gladys. 'All fur coat and no knickers that one.'

McFinn sat back with folded arms. 'My lips are sealed.'

'Well, that'll be the first time,' muttered Gertie, looking despondently at her empty bowl.

'We don't like to gossip about Lady Morag's guests,' chided Mrs Beesby. '… even the ones who might deserve it.'

'It all turned out for the good though,' said Bessie. 'Gave Miss Ophelia another go at reeling him in. We'll be making the cake for their wedding before long, just you see.'

Hettie, seated at one end of the table, pushed her bowl to one side, her syrup pudding uneaten.

Mrs Beesby rose and retied her apron. 'McFinn, you'd best be going up and giving Mr Haddock a hand setting up the mulled wine. Lady Morag will be ringing for us to join her round the tree, and you're still scraping the pattern off that bowl.'

'Too good to waste, Mrs Beesby. I never can resist a good portion of your puddings.'

'Saucy eejit,' she grumbled, tapping the back of his hand with a spoon.

DECK THE HALLS

7PM, CHRISTMAS EVE, 1928

OPHELIA DESCENDED the castle's grand staircase, her green silk gown kicking out with each step. She posed, arm on hip, midway, twisting to look back over her shoulder at Horatio, giving a provocative toss of her head.

He laughed. 'How perfectly lovely you look... and your hair is almost tidy for once! You must let me take your photograph later, darling.'

'You're too kind.' Ophelia smiled. She'd made extra efforts with her appearance, knowing Felicité would be pulling out all the stops. 'But, yes please. I might have it framed, and give it to Hamish.'

She looked up at the Christmas tree, glittering silver and gold, its lights the only ones twinkling in the Great Hall. 'It's a tradition that the family gathers round the tree on Christmas Eve. The servants too. There's mince pies and mulled wine, and carol singing. At home, Mummy gives our staff gifts on Boxing Day, but Granny's giving hers out tonight.'

'How quaint,' said Horatio. 'I expect all the best families do something similarly feudal.'

Pudding, crouched at Ophelia's feet, licked her lips, eying the gingerbread men freshly hung from the tree's lower branches, for the evening's activities.

Ophelia adjusted the position of one of the baubles. 'Morag wanted me to put on a white cloak and halo, can you believe, from the dressing-up box, and to lead us in a chorus of *Ding Dong Merrily on High*. Too, too shame-making, as if I'm nine years old, rather than twenty-one already.'

Horatio looked suitably alarmed. 'Horrors, darling! How did you get out of that?'

'Granny sent me up to one of the storage rooms in the servants' corridor to hunt out the costume and I simply pretended I couldn't find it. I located the trunks alright, but didn't bother to go delving.'

Ophelia nibbled at her nail. 'I felt rather uncomfortable, actually, as one of the maids is camping out in that room. It felt frightfully bad form, with her personal things being there. Not that she had much, but her night-gown was folded on her pillow, and her hairbrush was on the side. I tried not to look but I felt like a snoop.'

'Quite so, my dear. Everyone deserves their privacy.'

'Here they are,' called Morag, entering from the drawing room, a trail of guests in her wake. From the far corner, the servants also paraded in, the maids wearing clean aprons, and their caps sitting straight, under the vigilant eye of Mrs Beesby.

Ophelia recognised the Faucett-Plumbleys and several other neighbours. Lady Mildred set off across the hall at a lively clip, her granddaughter and husband in tow.

'Don't dilly-dally, Arthur,' she reprimanded her husband. 'I won't be left standing at the back.' Lord Faucett-Plumbley paused momentarily to accept a glass of mulled wine but his wife replaced it immediately upon the tray. 'I don't think so, Arthur.' She waggled her finger sternly. 'Sir Hector's concoctions are frightfully potent. You cannot have forgotten last year. The Countess of Sommersby was in a dreadful state after you grabbed her as you did.'

Ophelia swallowed a burst of laughter. 'Actually, she's quite right.' She stayed Horatio's arm as he went to sip from his glass. 'Hector's home-made wine is lethal. Best avoided.'

Hamish sidled up to them, pulling at his shirt cuffs beneath his jacket. 'I could do without all this dressing up,' he remarked, 'But I suppose it's worth it to see you in this gown.' He rested his hand upon Ophelia's waist and kissed her forehead.

'You both look ravishing.' Horatio cooed, his eyes swivelling to appraise them. 'I can see you perfectly as the next lord and lady of Castle Kintochlochie. Even if Hamish hasn't an official title, he has the respect that's due to one, which counts for rather more, I'd say.'

Ophelia barged Horatio gently, but Hamish smiled in thanks.

Lady MacKintoch clapped her hands to gain everyone's attention, giving her welcome, and leading them in the first carol of the evening: a rousing chorus of *Deck the Halls*. Ophelia winced a little, having Hector singing in one key to her left and the Colonel in another to her right. This was followed by a very jolly rendition of *Ding Dong Merrily on High*, Pudding offering up her own musical melody as those about her reached for the high notes.

Morag then presented each of the staff with a Christmas gift, Hector walking behind, muttering his own wishes for their good health in the coming year, and thanks for their service. Hamish followed, giving the female staff a chaste kiss on the cheek and shaking the men's hands.

'He's a real gentleman, he is,' sniffed Gertie. 'More than that Colonel, with his wandering hands, or Sir Hector. No matter that he looks a bit on the rough side when he's been staying in that forest cabin.'

'He's a good 'un alright,' agreed McFinn. 'No airs. Not like some of the toffs. Although I won't say nothing bad about Lady Morag, nor Lady Constance neither. They're good old birds.'

The trays of mince pies and mulled wine circulated again, the staff all taking their share, while Enid and Constance sang a duet of *Silent Night.* Their voices, though a little tremulous, were sweet, and they sang from the heart. Ophelia felt, for the first time, a responding quiver of excitement, sensing the magic of this special evening.

As they joined Morag in the final carol, *Away in a Manger,* Ophelia brushed away a small tear. Their own barns were full of animals. Not just horses, but the sheep and Highland cows, brought in out of the weather. They'd be relying on fodder while the snow lay thick and, with a blizzard forecast any day, it made sense to keep the livestock close. The horse Ophelia usually rode, Esmeralda, would soon be having her foal: a baby born into the hay, perhaps on this very night.

One day, Ophelia thought, I wouldn't mind having a baby.

She'd never particularly liked other people's but, looking up at Hamish, who'd returned to her side and was singing in a mellow baritone, she thought it might be rather wonderful.

The carol drawing to a close, Morag ushered her guests back to the drawing room. 'We've time for a quick cocktail before dinner,' she urged them. 'Must give Mrs Beesby time to ready her plates.'

Ophelia hung back, tilting her head to receive Hamish's kiss. 'I've hardly seen you all day,' she sighed, holding his hand in both her own. 'Not your fault, I know. You've been busy rounding up our four-legged assets. I'm sorry that I couldn't come and help.'

'It has been a long day,' he admitted. 'Better to be in the warm if you can. I'm used to these winters, while you're not. At least, not yet.' He kissed her hand and smiled wearily.

They were the last to enter the crowded room, but Félicité had clearly been waiting for them. She glided over, dazzling in a retina-popping silver sequinned gown, scooped low front and back. Ophelia, having just lifted a martini from a tray, was tempted to pop the olive from her drink into the clefted shelf of Felicité's bottom.

'Manhattans, darling!' declared Felicité, handing Hamish the cocktail from her own hand. 'I drink nothing else these days.'

'What's this?' blustered Hector. He sniffed his glass with suspicion. 'Mixing vermouth with my good whisky? Bloody sacrilege! Tell her, Hamish! And get me a proper drink while you're at it!'

'Don't worry Hector.' Hamish lead him to his favourite chair. 'Mr Worthington brought some American bourbon with him. I put your single malts out of the way this morning.'

'Good boy,' said Hector, somewhat mollified. 'Damn nuisance having all these strangers about the place, drinking my booze. Don't know why Morag bothers with them. Bunch of floozies and fornicators! And that young woman wearing barely a stitch of clothing; she'll catch her death!'

Hamish patted his shoulder soothingly.

Felicité wasted no time in following Hamish over, her husband tottering behind, finally lurching to grab the wing back of Hector's chair.

'Congratulations on your marriage,' said Hamish, shaking Wilberforce's hand and avoiding looking at Felicité altogether.

'Thank you, young man.' Wilberforce gave a smile comprising teeth that had most certainly not been grown in his own head. 'Never been to a British wedding before, or a genuine castle, so thought we'd swing by. Felicité was very keen.' He patted her bottom, and leered up at her. Wearing heels, she stood several inches above him.

'We'll be shooting some scenes for the latest movie over here: Felicité's playing Mary Queen of Scots. It'll be a great picture, especially with the authentic Edinburgh sets. We're heading that way as soon as we see Enid and her lucky groom get hitched.'

'They're not sets,' said Hamish, irritably. 'It's a real place, with real history.'

'Now, darling,' said Ophelia, coming over to lay her hand

proprietorially on his arm. She gave Felicité her most charming smile. 'I'm sure Mr Worthington doesn't mean to offend our beloved Scottish city. He's just viewing things through a director's eye.'

'Quite so, young lady. Everything here is so darned photogenic. Driving over here, I half expected Bonnie Prince Charlie to come riding over the mountains with his posse, broadsword swinging.'

Ophelia, hearing the gnash of Hamish's teeth, gave his elbow a squeeze. 'Just take it as a compliment, and let's change the subject, shall we?'

⁓

The gong sounded to call them into dinner, where there was much exclamation over the decoration of the table, which Ophelia had arranged. Holly and ivy trailed between eight candelabras, lit down its length. It had been set for thirty, with Kintochlochie's best crockery, in the family since the late 1700s. Crystal glassware sparkled and the silverware also caught the light, thanks to many hours of polishing.

Morag had planned the seating, placing Ophelia between the Colonel and Felicité's new husband. Hamish was opposite, between Marjorie and Enid.

As the first course arrived — a terrine of rabbit, Ophelia launched the conversation. 'Did you hear about the latest flight over Antarctica? Forty miles of previously uncharted territory mapped, and a territorial claim for the British government! Dreadfully exciting, although I wish there could have been a female pilot involved.'

'Oooh, yes,' agreed Marjorie. 'It's one of my ambitions to meet Amelia Earhart. Don't think I'd have the courage to ever get in a plane myself, mind you.'

'But it's safer to fly than to travel by sea,' interjected Felicité, from a little further down. 'We came over in the *Graf Zeppelin*. It is the only way I shall cross the Atlantic from now on.'

'Too right, baby,' said Wilberforce. 'Ships have been going down all over the place. First the *SS Vestris*, then the *RMS Celtic*. Not enough lifeboats, insufficient flares, and damned rocks waiting to shipwreck you off the coast of Ireland. You take your life in your hands every time you cross the gangway.'

'I sailed the Channel earlier this year, to go to St. Moritz,' enthused Marjorie. 'For the Winter Olympics! Jolly good show from the Norwegians, topping the medals table. Have you met Sonja Henie, Felicité, over in Hollywood? She took gold in the figure skating. I saw her in *Seven Days for Elizabeth* – lovely film!'

'I have not,' replied Felicité. 'I only mix with true stars, not sportswomen dabbling in the art of film. However, I was skiing in St. Moritz last Christmas, and found it delightful. My instructor, Helmut, is also a gold medallist. He does not usually take private clients, but gave many hours of private lessons to me. I have never conquered so many peaks.' She smiled smugly.

Ophelia found her attention drifting from one conversation to another as the next course arrived: roast goose with sage and chestnut stuffing, served with a parsnip purée and individual Yorkshire puddings.

'Splendid,' muttered the Colonel, shovelling a large forkful of meat into his mouth. 'Just as a young bird should be, what?'

His hand slipped beneath the table, giving Ophelia's thigh an excited squeeze. 'Damn good flesh; firm and moist.'

Ophelia was about to put down her cutlery and deal with the Colonel's over-eager fondling when she felt a second hand, this time from the other side. It was accompanied by the hot breath of Mr Worthington, panting against her bare arm.

'I enjoy your British-style stuffing,' he purred. 'I shall have to get the recipe, Lady Finchingfield. Or perhaps you'll show me how it's done.'

Ophelia caught a glance from Hamish, looking at her enquiringly across the table. She frowned, squinting to left and right, to which he responded by rolling his eyes.

Smiling all the while, Ophelia lowered her own hands, grasping the two offending appendages, now making headway in gathering the silk of her skirt upwards. Slowly, she brought them together. There was a kerfuffle in the vicinity of her lap, and then an abrupt intake of breath as the hands retreated, followed by embarrassed coughing from the Colonel.

'Can't blame me for trying, sweetie,' crooned Wilberforce, giving her the sort of wink that usually signified a seizure.

Ophelia was glad to see the sweet course arrive: a rich sherry trifle, brimming with fruit and cream.

It wasn't long before Morag stood, tinkling her spoon against her glass to command silence. 'I suggest we move through again, for our cognac and coffee. We have a selection of cheeses and petit fours, and then I shall be calling on you to join in with some party games.'

As they entered the drawing room once more, Ophelia watched Felicité shimmy over to her mother, extending her hand to introduce herself.

'We have something in common, I think,' said Felicité, giving a coquettish smile.

Lady Daphne's expression was cool, Ophelia noted, as she touched her fingers with those of the proffered hand.

'Our dresses,' went on Felicité, admiring Lady Daphne's gown, in deepest sapphire blue crêpe, with beaded chiffon sleeves. 'We have been to the same atelier in Paris, have we not?' She brushed, briefly, the long cuff at Lady Daphne's wrist. 'Such a pretty colour,' Felicité commented sweetly. 'And so elegant for a woman approaching what is, for us, a delicate age. There comes a time, does there not, when we must trade sex appeal for stateliness?'

Ophelia saw her mother stiffen, and her eyes flicker in steely fashion.

'We must all find our style,' Lady Daphne agreed. 'However, I fear you are still seeking yours, along with the rest of your dress.'

'If it gives pleasure for people to look, I shall offer them something worth seeing,' shrugged Felicité.

'Come on, Mummy,' said Ophelia, swooping in to take her mother's arm. 'Horatio wants to take a photo of our three generations of Castle Kintochlochie women. Next to the Christmas tree, I thought.'

MIDNIGHT MURDER

10PM, CHRISTMAS EVE, 1928

LADY MACKINTOCH STOOD upon a footstool and called out to the room at large. 'Now, my darlings. Some of us may be getting on in years, but there's life in us yet! I hope you're ready to join in with some party games.'

'Heaven help me,' muttered Lady Daphne. 'Think I'll slope off to bed.' She touched her husband's shoulder. 'I'll be waiting for you...'

Sir Peter knocked back his brandy in one gulp. 'No need to wait. I'm with you all the way.' He placed his arm about her waist. 'Lead on, my Lady, and don't spare the horses.'

'Peter! I do believe you're drunk,' she chastised as they made their way through the throng.

'Guilty as charged. I'm fully fuelled and on a count-down to launch.'

'Dreadful man!' She laughed, feeling the pinch of his fingers on her bottom.

'Blindman's Bluff to begin with,' declared Morag. 'We'll pop a sash around someone's eyes, spin them round, and see how many people they can identify by touch alone before the sand-timer ends.'

'What fun!' Felicité waved her hand to volunteer. 'I love being blindfolded!'

'Jolly good,' declared Morag. 'Gentlemen, don't be shy. We need you to form a circle around Mrs Worthington. And do remember not to give her any clues. No speaking!'

Hamish hung back; party games really weren't his thing. 'I see your parents have slipped away. I might do the same.' He nuzzled a kiss to Ophelia's neck. 'I need to check on Esmeralda anyway.'

Ophelia was about to suggest that they do so together when the Colonel took possession of Hamish's wrist.

'Come along! Morag wants to see us enjoying ourselves, so let's do our bit, shall we?' He led Hamish off, towards the circle. 'She won't bite, old thing!'

Horatio appeared at Ophelia's side. 'I wouldn't lay money on that.'

'She certainly is predatory,' conceded Ophelia, watching as Felicité reached out for the gentlemen surrounding her.

Felicité's blood-red nails skimmed over various bodies. Each time, she shook her head, asserting that she'd no idea who was before her.

Inevitably, she reached a certain tall specimen, resplendent in his kilted regalia. Her fingertips lingered upon his chest, unbuttoning his jacket, before reaching to stroke his bearded chin.

'Honestly!' complained Ophelia. 'She knows full well who she's gotten hold of. She's just dragging it out.'

'At least she hasn't put her hands under his kilt,' said Horatio. 'I wouldn't put it past her!'

'Time's up!' said Morag, holding the timer aloft. 'Time to swap! Ladies, form your circle please.'

Ophelia slunk back almost into the curtains. 'I'm not playing this game. It's no more than a glorified excuse for groping!'

'Quite right,' said Horatio. 'It would be far more efficient to turn us loose with the lights off and let everyone get on with it.'

Morag must have had the same idea, for the next game was Midnight Murder.

'Everyone needs to scatter,' she explained. 'Haddock will switch off the electricity at the main fuse box for the count of ten minutes. I've already chosen someone to be our villain. They'll stalk through the castle laying hands on their victims. We'll go around and count the 'bodies' when the lights go up again. More than five corpses and I'll award a prize!'

Horatio pulled a face. 'Quick! Let's get out of here while we can. Most of them will stampede for the bedrooms. I know what Morag's guests are like!'

Ophelia cast about, trying to locate Hamish. As Horatio scooted them across the hallway, she noticed some of the maids peeking from behind the kitchen service door, hiding their giggles. No doubt, they did all look rather comical. Only Hettie, the laundry maid, appeared strangely solemn. Lady Faucett-Plumbley was being pushed into the broom cupboard by the Colonel, both hands upon her ample bottom, while Flavia, the Faucett-Plumbley's granddaughter, had McFinn by the arm and was running in the direction of the library. Even Reverend McAdam and his wife were entering into the spirit of the game, dashing to conceal themselves behind the curtain on one side of the great door.

At last, Ophelia spotted Hamish, being guided towards the little door under the main staircase, in the clutches of Felicité. It was where they kept sports equipment: fishing and cricket paraphernalia, tennis racquets and golf clubs. Goodness knows how the two of them would fit in. Ophelia hoped a particularly large spider would be waiting to drop into Felicité's hair.

Hamish was frowning, looking around for her, she felt sure, but unable to sight her as others rushed past.

Horatio gave her another tug, and they disappeared into Hector's study. 'Hamish hid Hector's Port Ellen whisky in here,' he explained. 'Thirty years in the bottle! We can have a snifter while we're hiding.'

~

Cloaked in white, a hood obscuring its face, a figure glided silently along the deserted passageway on the second floor. Perhaps it took advantage of the castle, submerged in darkness; perhaps darkness was merely where it thrived. Reaching the balustrade of the gallery, it looked into the well of the Great Hall, then continued downwards.

As it moved towards the room on the far side, a sneeze from behind the curtains halted its progress momentarily.

'It's terribly dusty behind here. Really! Morag's staff must be a bit on the lazy side.'

On impulse, the mysterious figure leapt forward, wrenching the curtain and the two unfortunate guests hidden within its folds.

There was a shriek and a grunt from behind the faded velvet.

'Dash it Violet! You've given us away!

~

Pouring two generous tumblers of whisky, Horatio went to crouch behind the desk.

'You can forget that,' said Ophelia, stirring the glowing embers of the fire and then flopping onto the battered leather sofa. 'If we must play this silly game, I'd at least like to be comfortable. I'm lying here and our villain can come and murder me all he likes.'

'Fair enough,' said Horatio, standing to look out of the French Doors. 'Awfully pretty round here, I must say. I've not seen moonlight on fresh snow before. You'll have to help me round them up for a group photo tomorrow, Ophelia, at the front of the castle.'

Ophelia yawned and nodded, closing her eyes.

~

Horatio had refilled his glass, and once more secreted himself behind the desk when the handle of the study door turned.

The room was quiet, lit only by the glow from the dying fire.

Ophelia shifted upon the sofa, and the figure stepped forward.

Swiftly, the figure swept up a folded woollen blanket and flung the cloth over Ophelia's head, then shook her shoulders hard, pressing down with all their might.

Ophelia shrieked and flayed, her feet kicking.

'I say!' Horatio exclaimed, sloshing his drink as he struggled to stand up. 'Who goes there?'

The figure fled across the room, flicking the latch on the French Doors and disappearing into the night.

~

'Damnation!' cried Ophelia, at last finding her way out from beneath the blanket. 'Bloody uncivilized!'

Horatio rushed to her side. 'Are you alright?'

'I am, but no thanks to whoever that was. Taking their job as the Midnight Murderer far too seriously! They've quite wrenched my neck. I shall have bruises tomorrow!'

Horatio helped her sit up.

'Are you sure that's what it was? I caught sight of it briefly. All in white.'

With hands slightly trembling, Horatio picked up Ophelia's untouched glass and drained her inch of whisky. His voice was barely above a whisper.

'Do you think Lady Daphne was right? That there was a ghostly presence in her room? What I saw had the air of something from beyond the grave...'

Ophelia took the glass from Horatio and set it down on the table. 'Between the cocktails, wine and whisky, your judgement isn't to be trusted. Besides which, I don't believe in supernatural rubbish. I've been here half the year, remember. There's never been a hint of anything otherworldly.'

'Perhaps the ghost only appears at Christmas,' insisted Horatio.

'Nonsense!' Ophelia interjected. 'Which way did they go?'

'I saw the edge of its cloak as it departed out into the snow – through the French Doors.'

As she leaned out to reach the handle, her gaze fell onto the snow beneath, and she beckoned to Horatio.

'Ghosts don't leave footprints, do they?'

HIDE AND SEEK

AFTER 11PM, CHRISTMAS EVE, 1928

OPHELIA STRODE INTO THE HALL, calling out to Hamish.

'Shhh!' urged Horatio, hot on her heels. 'The ghost might still be about!'

'Never mind that,' said Ophelia. 'I need to find Hamish.'

There was enough light coming through the windows either side of the great door for Ophelia to make her way easily to the little cupboard beneath the stairs. She yanked the door open and Hamish spilled out, as if he'd been pushing hard from the other side.

'Thank Christ for that,' he announced. 'Bloody door was stuck, and no handle on the inside. Thought we'd be in there overnight!'

Felicité unfolded herself from within, smoothing her hair and pulling up the strap of her dress. 'Thank you, darling.' She stroked Hamish's arm. 'It was fun while it lasted, but I don't recommend this as the place for a rendezvous.'

She turned to Ophelia with a simpering smile. 'Poor Hamish is so huge! He did his best to remain upright, but it was an awful squeeze.'

Ophelia turned to Hamish, her eyes filled with hurt. She didn't trust herself to speak.

Hamish had just taken a step towards her when there was a piercing scream from upstairs. A door banged, and there were raised voices, followed by running footsteps.

A hand gripped Ophelia's from behind; she could feel Horatio trembling.

'What the blazes!' Hamish was halfway up the stairs when the lights came on, revealing Hector standing at the top, wearing his nightshirt and shaking with fury.

'Just found three of them in my bed!' he spluttered.

'Calm down, Hector,' soothed Hamish. 'Let's get you back to your room.'

'Damn cheek! Fornicating like rutting animals! No better than a brothel!'

'Is that all?' Felicité appeared highly amused. 'I thought there had been at least a murder.'

'Knowing Hector, there very well could have been,' said Ophelia. 'Anyway, it's certainly not funny for him. He ought to be able to climb into his bed without finding other people already in it.'

Felicité waved her fingers airily. 'Whatever you say, darling…'

~

'She's a succubus!' raged Ophelia, kicking her shoes off so violently that one of them clattered against her bedroom wall. Pudding yelped and dived under the bed. 'She came out of that cupboard looking like the cat that got the cream, and minus most of her lipstick.'

Ophelia unclipped her earrings and flung them onto the dressing table. 'I trust you, of course, but how can you have been so foolish? She'll be thinking that she only has to snap her fingers and you're at her beck and call.' Ophelia felt a sob rising. 'It's humiliating!'

Hamish hugged her to him, stroking her hair. She struggled for a moment, then let herself relax against his chest, allowing her tears of frustration to flow.

'It's alright, I've calmed myself,' she said at last, pulling away, then perching on her dressing table stool. She wiped her cheeks.

Hamish knelt beside her and took her hand. 'Nothing happened,' he said simply. 'But I'm sure you already know that. I shouldn't have let Felicité manipulate me, dragging me off to hide. Believe me, it was the last thing I wanted.'

As he rubbed his eyes, Ophelia realized how tired he looked. He'd been working long hours for weeks now, training the estate workers in new forestry techniques while undertaking all his usual duties, and keeping an eye on the new livestock.

'Forgive me.' Ophelia smiled weakly. 'I'm being over-sensitive. I've definitely had more to drink that I should have and I had a bit of a fright while Horatio and I were hiding in Hector's study. I'll feel better about it in the morning.'

Hamish frowned. 'What is it, darling? Are you alright?'

'I will be.' She massaged her neck. 'Our Midnight Murderer was rather over-zealous, that's all.'

They both rose, and she turned to let him unzip her gown.

'Come to bed,' she whispered, letting the silk slither to the floor.

He brought his mouth to hers and wrapped her tight as he kissed her. She knew that his body would be stirred by her warmth.

'I'm expecting Esmeralda to have her foal tonight.' He sighed. 'I need to stay with her. Murray's a good lad but he's still learning, and the head groom has had to leave for Fort William; his mother's unwell.'

'That's too bad.' Ophelia twined her arms about his neck. She loved the feel of him, fully clothed, against her bare skin. She ached for him, as she always did, and knew he was reluctant to leave her. 'Once the foal comes, you'll slip back, won't you? Don't worry about the time.'

Hamish rested his head against hers. 'I won't want to wake you. One of us might as well get our full quota of sleep.'

He led her to the bed and tucked her under the covers. 'I'd better change and go down. Get your rest, Ophelia, and I'll see you in the morning.'

When he'd gone, she realized that she hadn't locked the door. She rose to turn the key before climbing back into bed.

❧

It was well after midnight when Pudding opened a single eye, the other remaining dedicated to the simulation of sleep. Someone was in the room. Someone whose smell was not unfamiliar to Pudding, but whose presence was unexpected.

She began with a warning growl. When the figure approached the bed, she moved on swiftly to full-throttle barking. Was it possible that such a ferocious racket could issue from the lungs of one small terrier? Yes – if the terrier in question was Pudding, and her mistress was in danger.

The ghostly figure made its departure.

'Pudding, what's the matter? Who are you barking at?' mumbled Ophelia, rubbing the sleep from her eyes.

She reached for the lamp on her bedside, twisted the flame into life, and held it aloft.

The room was dark and cold. She could see her own breath. A shiver of fear passed over her.

'Is Hamish at the door?'

Rising to open it, Ophelia found that it was still locked, the key in her own side, untouched. She listened carefully.

'There's no one, except perhaps a mouse in the skirting. Is that what you heard, little Pudding?' She scratched the terrier fondly behind the ears. 'Now, back in bed before we freeze! I'm bringing you under the covers with me, so no squirming. It's the least you can do, having woken me up.'

Despite herself, it took some time for Ophelia to fall back to sleep.

VIOLENCE IN THE NIGHT

EARLY MORNING, CHRISTMAS DAY, 1928

OPHELIA WAS ROUSED by a persistent rap.

'I've your tray, M'Lady.'

Ophelia recognized Mary's voice and hurried over to turn the key.

'I wouldn't have brought you from your bed, M'Lady, but I couldn't open the door,' Mary apologized.

'My fault,' said Ophelia, scurrying back to the warmth of the covers. 'Foolish of me, I know. After the fright my mother had, I thought I'd lock myself in.' She hugged her knees, not wanting to say anything about what had happened in Hector's study. 'Of course, if a castle ghost is roaming, I don't suppose a locked door will make much difference...'

'No, M'Lady.' Mary touched a match to the kindling laid ready in the hearth. 'The frost was hard in the night, so you'd best wear the warmer of your dresses. The red wool?'

'Yes please, Mary,' said Ophelia, sipping her hot chocolate. 'And Happy Christmas to you!'

'And to you, Lady Ophelia.' Mary gave her a broad smile. 'I'll put the dress near the fire to warm, and your thermal vest too.'

Mary stooped to pick up the green silk dress Ophelia had been wearing the night before, and which lay still on the floor, where she had dropped it. As Mary shook it out, she gasped.

'Oh, M'Lady, what's happened?'

It was torn from the hem upwards, in a fierce rent.

'Did you catch it on something, M'Lady?' asked Mary. 'I'm afraid not even my needle will be able to fix this.'

Ophelia felt a chill that had nothing to do with the temperature of the room. She looked about her.

'Mary, check my jewel box, would you. Is my diamond clip there?'

Doing as she was bid, Mary opened the casket.

'Yes, M'Lady. It's here, and everything else.'

Not that there is much else, thought Ophelia. I only have my lovely hair clip because granny gave it to me from her own box.

'And the window, Mary, is it latched?'

Mary checked, then nodded her confirmation.

'I don't know what happened to the dress.' Ophelia frowned. 'I was sleepy last night, and I'd had more to drink than was sensible. Perhaps I did catch the hem and tear it, without noticing. I'm sorry. It seems a shame to throw it away. Perhaps, when you have time, you might cut it down and make a blouse or something...?'

'I'm sure I can do that, M'Lady,' said Mary, giving a bob.

Alone again, Ophelia clutched Pudding to her chest. Someone, or something, had been in the room, and had destroyed her favourite gown. Not a thief, for they would surely have taken the hair clip. Not a person at all, perhaps, for how had they entered her room, with the door and window locked.

~

Once dressed, Ophelia bundled Pudding under her arm, and crossed the hall to knock upon Hamish's door. There was no reply. Pushing it open, she saw the bed hadn't been slept in. He must have stayed all night in the stables.

'Horatio, are you awake?' she hissed, padding to his door, further along the passage.

'It's open,' answered a groggy voice.

'My goodness, what time is it?' yawned Horatio, reaching for his clock. 'Not even eight o'clock! My dear, what's going on? I usually take my beauty sleep until at least nine.'

Ophelia locked the door behind her, and sat upon the bed. Pudding leapt up too and rolled on her back. Horatio was usually attentive in the tummy-rub department.

It didn't take long for Ophelia to relate all that had happened: Pudding's behaviour in the night, and the damage to her dress.

'How extraordinary! And you say both the door and window were locked! Then, it's impossible that someone entered.' Horatio looked uneasy. 'Unless, there really is a ghost!'

'Enough of that, Horatio,' said Ophelia. 'There must be a rational explanation. Pudding might have heard an owl at the window, or come nose-to-nose with a rat. Meanwhile, I was rather tipsy. I could have caught the silk on one of the bannisters as I ran upstairs. There are quite a few stray splinters.'

Ophelia pulled gently on Pudding's rear paws, trying to make sense of it all. 'Although, you'd think I'd have noticed, or Hamish might have done...'

'You were in rather a foul mood with the poor man,' Horatio observed. 'Perhaps he didn't like to mention it, for fear of another tongue-lashing.'

'No more than he deserved. And as for that vixen...'

'We can hardly blame our dear Mrs Worthington. Her husband doesn't look capable of much. If I was in a cupboard with Hamish I don't think I'd be able to keep my hands to myself either.'

'Nothing happened!' said Ophelia, feeling a wave of irritation return.

'Of course not...' Horatio was quiet for a moment, then gave Pudding a playful tickle.

'It is all rather odd, though.' He mused, returning to their previous train of thought. 'Your mother waking, swearing she's seen an apparition; and then the ghostly figure attacking you last night, while we were in Hector's study; and now your dress.'

Ophelia gave herself a little shake. 'I'll forget all about it, Horatio. It's Christmas Day, for which I shall give you a kiss, and we have the festivities of the day to look forward to.'

'It is, my dear. Happy Christmas to you.' Horatio reached to the drawer of his bedside cabinet. 'I have a gift for you, which you should open now, and then enjoy for the rest of the day.'

The package was small, wrapped in gold tissue paper, with a silver ribbon. 'It's from one of the Parisian flea markets.' Horatio blushed. 'No value to speak of, but I knew you'd like it. It will go very well with your dress.'

Ophelia exclaimed in delight, for the brooch was perfect: an oval of amethyst, framed in tiny seed pearls.

'I've something for you too, Horatio, but I'll wait until later, when you're dressed.' Ophelia jumped up from the bed. 'For now, I'm going to wrap up as warmly as I can and go out to the stables, where I expect I'll find someone ready for a flask of hot coffee.'

A CHRISTMAS BREAKFAST

ABOUT 8AM, CHRISTMAS DAY, 1928

'FRIED HAM AND TATTIE SCONES? It must be Christmas!' said McFinn, sliding into his seat at the kitchen table. 'To your health, Mrs Beesby!' He raised his tea cup and gave her one of his grins.

'And Merry Christmas to you, McFinn. If we can't have a good breakfast on this day of the year, when can we?'

'Too right!' McFinn leaned in to sniff the platter.

'Are those scrambled eggs done, Susan?' asked Mrs Beesby, taking off her apron. 'You can put the skillet straight on the slate here and we'll all dig in.'

Bessie, Gertie and Gladys were already seated on one side. They'd been up since five o'clock, clearing abandoned glassware and laying new fires downstairs, and lighting those in the bedrooms. They were ready for their breakfasts.

'Mr Haddock will be here in a moment. He's just taken up Sir Hector's tray. And I've already sent a message to Murray, in the stables.'

'Ah, there you are Hettie,' said Mrs Beesby, seeing her come in. 'I've a notion you've overslept this morning, but I'll overlook it, seeing as it's the day of the Lord's birth.'

Hettie took her seat quietly amidst the hubbub of the other servants' chatter.

'You look right exhausted!' said Gladys. 'Is it that camp bed in the storage room, keeping you awake?'

'Something like that,' Hettie admitted, holding out her cup to be filled.

'We'll save a plate for Ethel.' Mrs Beesby spooned some eggs out. 'She's getting her appetite back, so we'll make sure it's a good portion. Put that in the oven to warm, Susan, and this one for Mrs Worthington's maid. We'll take them up afterwards.'

Gertie gave a sniff. 'Too good to come down and eat with the likes of us, that Adelina. I'd leave hers to go cold.'

'Now, now,' chided Mrs Beesby. 'That's not in the spirit of the day, is it? If Mrs Wilberforce's maid wishes to eat separately from us, then that's her choice.'

'Snooty cow,' mumbled Gertie.

'I'm not too late, am I?' Mary scurried in. 'I've dressed Lady Morag and need to go up for Lady Constance as soon as I've grabbed a bite.'

With everyone finally making their way to the table, breakfast began in earnest. Mrs Beesby looked round in satisfaction at the assembled staff, tucking happily into her cooking. Mr Beesby had departed this world before she'd had the chance for children of her own, but she thought of the young women as the daughters she might have had. She had a soft spot for McFinn too, cheeky though he was.

'There's enough for three potato scones each, so don't be shy,' said the cook. 'We won't be eating again until Upstairs is enjoying the Wedding buffet, laid out in the ballroom. Lady Morag said we can take half an hour. Mr Haddock just needs to leave sufficient champagne poured, and they'll help themselves. Like a picnic, Lady Morag says.'

'Too generous, I'm sure,' grumbled Gertie.

'What's put you in such a bad mood?' asked Gladys. 'It's Christmas, isn't it? You've had your present from Lady Morag and we'll have goose and all the trimmings later. There won't be many having such a good feed today.'

'A bar of lavender soap and some new hankies are all very well, but we're still expected to run after them at all hours. I wouldn't mind a day to put my feet up, for once.' Gertie chewed aggressively on her ham.

'Then you'd best find someone rich enough to keep you,' Bessie interjected.

'Rich enough and blind enough!' sniggered McFinn.

'Oi!' Gertie scowled.

'My ears are still sharp enough to hear what happens at that end of the table,' warned Mrs Beesby. 'Just remember, girls, that our bride and groom today are far from in the first flush of youth.'

'True words,' agreed Mr Haddock, giving Mrs Beesby the warmest of smiles. 'It's never too late for love!'

MOONSHINE

ALSO ABOUT 8AM, CHRISTMAS DAY, 1928

As Ophelia approached the stables, carrying a flask and some potato scones, wrapped in a cloth by Mrs Beesby, Murray was just coming out.

'Happy Christmas, M'Lady,' said Murray, touching his cap. 'Esmeralda's done well. It's a bonny little foal. Mr Hamish is with them, in the far stall.'

Ophelia returned the festive greeting and smiled shyly. More than once, Murray had come upon them kissing. Everyone in the house seemed aware that she and Hamish were fond of each other, but they'd tried to be discreet — difficult as that was in a house brimming with relatives, guests and servants.

'Mrs Beesby's breakfast is nearly ready, Murray. Do go ahead.' She indicated the provisions in her arms. 'I'm just taking these to Hamish.'

'Right you are, M'Lady.'

Murray ran off across the yard and Ophelia hurried into the

stables. Although the sun was shining, the air was chill. A slight breeze stirred the powered snow.

Inside, the heat and tang of six horses filled the confined space. The sour-sweet scent of their bodies mixed with that of the hay and fresh manure. Each beast turned to her as she passed, eager to have its nose stroked, and to see whether she'd brought a treat in her pocket.

Hearing Ophelia's voice, Hamish came out of Esmeralda's stall. The straw attached to his clothing, and in his beard, bore evidence of his rough bedding-down. He inclined his head, inviting her to look in at the filly and her new foal.

'I thought you might like to choose a name.'

Esmeralda gazed over her shoulder at Ophelia, giving a gentle whinny. Her foal, a deep chestnut, with a blaze of white on all four feet, suckled beneath her belly.

'She's a beauty. Well done Hamish.' Ophelia hugged him excitedly. 'And well done, Esmeralda.'

'The foal arrived at about five this morning,' said Hamish, watching as Ophelia poured the steaming coffee. 'Delivery took a bit longer than usual, but it went well once I'd gotten the front legs through.'

Ophelia invited Hamish to take a scone, but he put down his cup, and wrapped her tightly to him. She'd intended to ask him about her green silk gown, to see if he'd noticed the tear the night before. With his arms around her, it suddenly seemed silly. Of course, it had been an accident. She must have caught the hem herself.

She raised her mouth to his and they stood for some time, neither wishing to break off from their kiss, warm in each other's arms.

'Merry Christmas,' she said, at last, tipping her head back and smiling, then making a show of holding her nose at the smell of him, which was akin to that of the horses, overlaid with his own sweat, from the labour of helping Esmeralda birth her foal. 'My goodness, Hamish, you might want to bathe before you dress for church.'

Hamish laughed, but his eyes were suddenly serious.

'I've never been happier than I am now,' he told her. 'Please know that I want to spend my life with you, and I hope you'll return that desire. I want you to believe that I'll care for you, to know that I'll always look after your happiness.'

He skimmed her hairline with his mouth, then whispered into the cradle of her ear.

'I want you to give yourself wholly to me, Ophelia.'

Unbuttoning her coat, his hands moved over her breasts, and then behind, stroking her back lightly through the red wool dress.

'I want your body,' he confided, pressing her closer to him, 'But not only that. I want your mind and your heart. I want your trust.'

She was tempted, for a moment, to give up her struggle, to allow him to take charge of her. She'd given so much of herself, allowed him to see so much. Couldn't she have faith in him? Believe that he'd keep his word and love her truly, without ever hurting her?

Something in her still fought against the idea; some part of her trembled, doubting and afraid. Ophelia drew back, and felt his hands release her.

However, Hamish continued to look at her tenderly. He took something from his pocket.

'It was my mother's.'

He tipped a ring from a small pouch. The band was silver, set with a moonstone.

'I know I've not always behaved well, and I don't blame you for being cautious, but please know that I love you, Ophelia. I want you to be my wife.'

He took her left hand in his, holding the ring a few inches from her fingers.

'It's beautiful, Hamish.' It was difficult to keep her tone steady. 'I love you, too. You know I love you.' She felt the prickle of tears, threatening to overcome her. 'I will say yes, soon. I know I will.' She struggled to find the words. 'Until then, can I wear it on the other hand?'

Her pulse fluttered with fear, awaiting his look of reproach. She'd no wish to wound him, no desire to punish him for having let her down before. It was the dictate of her heart that she followed. She wanted to be sure before she made her promise.

'My darling,' he murmured, folding her into his chest again. 'Of course.' She detected a thickness in his voice. 'I shouldn't have asked; it's too soon, and it's not right for me to rush you.'

'But I like being asked.' She looked up at him, through the tears she could no longer hold back. 'I really do.'

She held her hand out to accept the ring. He fumbled a little, all fingers and thumbs, but it fitted almost perfectly, only a little loose past her knuckle.

'Moonshine,' said Ophelia. 'Let's call the new foal Moonshine — for her white feet and this beautiful stone.'

Hamish nodded, raising Ophelia's hand to receive his kiss.

'Now, shall we get you inside, Hamish? They'll all be waiting, and you absolutely must wash before you're presentable.' Ophelia laughed, wiping her damp cheeks.

In response, he cupped his arm under her legs and lifted her into the air, carrying her to the end of the stable, where the clean hay was stacked, ready to feed the horses.

'I'm not quite finished with you yet,' he said softly, laying her down. His hands were warm, as they slid upwards, beneath her dress.

STRANGE REVELATIONS

9.30AM, CHRISTMAS DAY, 1928

OPHELIA HEARD the chatter from the breakfast room even before pushing open the door. Despite the late hours kept by the party the night before, almost everyone had gathered, lured perhaps by the mouth-watering smell of bacon. Mrs Beesby had sent up not only the usual cooked breakfast items, but fragrant kedgeree and a platter of smoked fish.

She hoped that Hamish wouldn't be long in coming down. She knew kedgeree was his favourite.

Earlier, in her state of agitation, Ophelia had thought she wouldn't be able to eat a bite but she found now that she was ravenous. She did a lap of the table, giving various kisses and exchanging Christmas greetings, before filling her plate with a kipper and soft scrambled eggs. She wondered if it would be greedy to add a couple of sausages.

Pudding stationed herself to one end of the buffet, eyes peeled for any stray morsel than might hit the floor.

Felicité was wearing a beautifully cut dress in emerald green this morning, with black embroidery through the yoke and at her cuffs. As ever, her blonde hair was coiffed impeccably. She lifted the lid of one of the silver tureens.

'No wonder all these women have the enormous *derrieres*,' she said irritably, directing her observation to Ophelia's ears. 'So much butter, and cream! And all this meat! I shall just have some toasted bread with sautéed mushrooms.'

She snapped her fingers at Haddock, who was pouring champagne for the merry crowd. It wasn't a usual breakfast drink at Castle Kintochlochie but, being Christmas, and the day of Enid and the Colonel's wedding, Morag had obviously decided to push the boat out. McFinn was at the other end of the room, with the coffee pot.

'I cannot eat these eggs,' said Felicité imperiously. 'Ask the kitchen to send some up for me, poached, and more tomatoes. These are cold.'

Ophelia rubbed her thumb against the ring newly placed upon her finger and smiled to herself. She could afford to be generous-hearted. It was she that Hamish loved, and not Felicité.

Ophelia asked sympathetically if she had a headache.

'I do,' Felicité admitted, 'But not from the cocktails or champagne. It is the wallpaper in my room that has given me this dreadful head. If I sleep in there another night, it will bring on insanity.' She stabbed at the smoked salmon, lifting several pieces onto her plate. She sighed deeply. 'I may have to share with Wilberforce.'

Horatio had saved Ophelia a seat beside him. Lady Faucettt-Plumbley, resplendent in a pleated skirt of orange crepe, paired with a mustard-yellow blouse, and wearing one of her better wigs, was opposite, chatting animatedly with Reverend McAdam's wife. They seemed to be getting along rather well.

'I don't know how Mr Worthington can bear to be married to such a flashy strumpet,' she was saying. 'The size of the diamond on her finger! Ridiculously vulgar!' She chewed vigorously on a mixed forkful of breakfast delights, then dabbed delicately at her mouth with a napkin. 'I've told Flavia not to engage with her in any fashion. Sixteen is such an impressionable age.'

Flavia, seated to her grandmother's other side, was looking rather dreamily down the room at McFinn, Ophelia noticed. It didn't look as though she needed Felicité's help to be lead astray.

As Lady Faucett-Plumbley rose to replenish her plate, Felicité sauntered down and slipped into her place. She smiled sweetly at Mrs McAdam and dropped her voice, as if to speak confidentially. 'Wearing such horrible clothes is bound to put one in an unfortunate mood, isn't it?'

Felicité popped a button-mushroom between her crimson lips and winked at Ophelia.

Lady McKintoch's voice carried down the table, talking of a subject which made Ophelia prick up her ears.

'I hope everyone enjoyed our games last night. Hiding in cupboards always reminds me of my debutante days.' The tray of champagne appeared at her right shoulder, and she helped herself to another glass. 'Mr Worthington was our Midnight Murderer and swears he only managed to find three victims before his hip went — the Colonel and Lady Faucett-Plumbley, and dear old Hector, who'd fallen asleep in a chair and didn't manage to hide at all.' Morag paused for a sip of fizz. 'Except, of course, that the McAdams tell me they were also pounced upon, behind the hall curtain, which makes five corpses! Most strange!'

Horatio gripped Ophelia's arm. 'With you, that's six!'

Ophelia put down her fork. Her appetite had suddenly vanished.

Pudding had come to lie at Ophelia's feet, knowing that a bit of something tasty was likely to make its way under the table if she were patient. However, as one of the maids entered, coming to whisper in Mr Haddock's ear that the special order of poached eggs was ready and she'd placed them upon the cabinet, Ophelia's faithful terrier took a different stance altogether.

Pudding sniffed the air and emitted a growl. In one giant leap, she raced across the room, her nose doing double-duty, examining the maid's ankle.

'Oh! I don't like it!' shrieked the owner of the leg, kicking her foot at the terrier's plump little body.

'Be careful, Hettie! You'll hurt her!' reprimanded Ophelia, jumping up to lift Pudding into her arms. 'There are enough dogs in the house. You really should be used to them by now, and there's no reason for them to attack you, so do calm down.'

Hettie, having drawn all eyes to her, looked terrified, as if one and all were about to rise and assail her. She fled from the room with a sob. Haddock and McFinn exchanged worried glances.

Morag rose and clapped her hands. 'If you've all finished, it might be an idea for us to dress for the chapel, since we'll be heading over in less than an hour. Constance and Mary are with Enid. Horatio, perhaps you'd go with the Colonel, to help him into his morning suit? Hamish is standing as best man, but must be waylaid somewhere. We might exchange gifts later, before the evening party begins.'

As the others left, Ophelia drew Lady Morag to one side, still clutching Pudding to her chest.

'Granny, I must ask you something,' she began. 'I've learnt a great deal about Castle Kintochlochie since I came here, but I wondered if there's something I might be unaware of... some old legend, or something else, anything odd, or unexplainable.'

'My dear, you're shaking,' said Morag, guiding Ophelia to take a seat. 'It's not like you to be troubled by thoughts of this kind.'

'Can you think of anything unusual?' Ophelia insisted. If there was a ghost haunting the castle, she'd rather know as much as she could.

Morag considered for a moment. 'Not that I can think of, my

dear, but old buildings have their secrets, don't they, just like the people who inhabit them.'

'You've never seen a ghost, or heard tell of one?'

'Oh, there are lots of stories,' said Morag, waving her hand dismissively. 'The headless laird who's supposed to haunt the ball-room, still brandishing his sword from battle, and they say that the spirit of some poor serving girl walks near the loch. There are all the usual tales about changelings and faeries and hobgoblins, but I've never seen anything myself. I'm not one for entertaining such nonsense, and I didn't think you were, Ophelia.'

'No, of course not.' Ophelia shook her head, but her eyes looked uncertain.

Morag saw now how pale Ophelia was, and the slight shadow beneath her eyes, as if she hadn't slept properly.

'Has something frightened you, Ophelia? You looked perfectly happy when you came in earlier but, now, you don't look so well.'

'Oh, it's nothing really.' Ophelia attempted to laugh. 'A few 'bumps in the night', and a couple of things I can't explain.'

She'd no intention of worrying Morag by telling her that someone had half-strangled her in the study, and that she'd woken to find her dress torn so strangely.

Of course, she didn't believe in ghosts. Someone was up to mischief. It was the only explanation. And the attacks weren't directed at her alone. Hadn't her mother been the first to be assailed? And two other guests had also fallen foul of whoever had come into the study. She just needed to be brave. The mischief-maker would soon get bored if they refused to show fear.

That's how it was in all the best novels. The heroine had to show her mettle, and all would come right in the end. Ophelia hoped there was something in it.

VOWS OF LOVE

10.30AM, CHRISTMAS DAY, 1928

THE CHAPEL HAD that particular smell Ophelia always associated with old churches: dust and wood polish, and the mustiness of books which have sat too long in the cold and damp. Situated in the grounds behind Castle Kintochlochie, overlooking the walled garden and the rising mountains that surrounded the tranquil valley, the chapel had stood for almost as long as the castle itself, welcoming the Faithful to its sacred masses.

Though unheated, Morag and Constance had done their best to ensure the comfort of their guests, placing cushions and blankets along each pew. A portable, wood-burning stove had been set up early that morning, but did little to remove the chill; Ophelia was able to see her breath as she gazed up at the chapel's vaulted ceiling. Hewn from trees which must once have breathed upon the Kintochlochie hillsides, the rafters were ornately carved, depicting stags and does, hares and hunting birds.

She'd done her part, decorating the deep window sills and the altar with trailing ivy, mistletoe and holly branches, the greenery offsetting berries pearly white and crimson. Candles burned in brass candlesticks, their flames flickering at the end of each pew, serving as the only illumination in the ancient gathering place, but for the weak December light filtering through the simple leaded windows.

Ophelia pulled her coat tighter, snuggling her face into the fur stole about her neck. She tapped her feet together, wriggling her cold toes and wishing, not for the first time, that she had warmer outerwear. Her mother, sitting in the front left pew, beside Ophelia's father, Lady Morag and Lady Constance, was wearing full fur, in dark grey mink, including a large hat, and looked far more comfortable.

The Colonel stood stiffly at the front, awaiting his bride, Hamish at his side, looking considerably smarter than he had done in the stable. He'd given the groom a horseshoe for luck, before they'd walked over, along the path Murray had cleared through the snow. Ophelia could see the Colonel fingering it, inside his pocket, as if anxious that Enid might have a change of heart and leave him jilted at the altar. It hardly seemed likely. They were as in love as Ophelia had seen any two people, despite the Colonel's occasional wandering hands.

The chapel was filled with quite a few people Ophelia didn't know, although their faces were somewhat familiar, from Morag's summer birthday party.

'You'd think people would want to spend Christmas Day quietly at home, with their families, wouldn't you?' Ophelia remarked to Horatio, seated beside her.

'Good Heavens! No!' Horatio laughed at the thought. 'The last people I'd want to be with at Christmas are my own family. I had an invitation from the Beatons, the dears. Cecil is always such fun. They'll be playing charades and singing around the piano and making the most fantastic cocktails.'

He looked thoughtful for a minute. 'I'll be with them at New

Year instead. I know I'm always welcome. They care for me more than my own family, of that I'm certain.'

Ophelia leaned in to whisper. 'I know what you mean. Daddy loves me, but I often think Mummy only cares in so far as I might throw her into a good light. If I don't marry someone she approves of, I fear she won't bother with me at all anymore.'

'What a pair we are,' lamented Horatio. 'Although I have to say that your family is infinitely nicer than mine. Lady Morag dotes on you, and even your mother isn't the monster you imagine. She only wants what's best for you. It's just that she's judging by a very particular set of criteria for happiness.'

Ophelia managed a smile.

'Oh, look!' Horatio exclaimed, as Mrs McAdam struck up the first chords of *The Wedding March*. 'It's Enid, and she's ravishing.'

The ivory chiffon dress, flowing almost to the floor, suited Enid's complexion marvellously. Accented with a cream sash just below the natural waistline and pearls sewn into the hem and yoke, it was understated, yet elegant. She carried a slender bouquet of apricot-coloured roses, interspersed with mistletoe and ivy, while her veil, reaching to the hemline of her gown, was clasped either side of her head with silk roses in the same shade. Her hair, recently bobbed, and now set in a fashionable wave, remained a rich auburn, thanks to the regular application of a little bottle of magic. Marjorie followed behind, in a simple apricot shift, holding a smaller bouquet.

'How radiant Enid looks,' agreed Ophelia. 'She's fit to burst with happiness.'

'True enough!' said Horatio. 'No matter what we think of the Colonel, he's making her delirious in the romantic stakes.'

Ophelia rubbed his arm. 'It'll be you some day.'

'Walking down the aisle?' scoffed Horatio. 'Hardly, my dear. Unless they repeal the laws of the land and allow those like me to marry who they truly love.' He extracted his handkerchief and blew his nose. 'I don't think I could bring myself to marry just to please my family. Mind you, they've stopped trying to introduce me to nice young women.' He managed a smile. 'Realized I'm a lost cause.'

Ophelia squeezed Horatio's hand. 'Well, maybe not quite like this, but you'll find your Prince Charming. Perhaps, you already have... someone behind a certain camera?'

'Ridiculous girl,' said Horatio, dabbing at his eyes, but returning the pressure of her hand.

The bride arrived beside her groom, looking up at him in a way that made Ophelia's heart leap; her own eyes rested upon Hamish's shoulders, and the tumble of his ginger hair, curling at the nape of his neck.

Reverend McAdam's voice rang out across the pews. 'Let our hearts be filled with joy on this Christmas morning, as we celebrate Christ's birth. We gather here for the matrimony of Montague Faversham and Enid Ellingmore. May they bring happiness to each other, within the bond of wedlock, and to all who know them.'

He opened his arms upon the congregation and the bride and groom. 'Now, let's begin by singing *Hark the Herald Angels Sing*. A song reminding us of the eternal hope and light which blazes inside us all.'

The Reverend nodded to his wife, who was seated at the little organ to one side, and the pipes burst into the first notes of the melody.

Once Hamish had fulfilled his duty of passing the rings to the Colonel, he slipped into the pew on Ophelia's other side, putting his arm about her waist and pulling her close. Although they were partially concealed behind one of the chapel's eight stone columns, Ophelia was aware of others' eyes upon them, including Lady Daphne's if she cared to turn her head. Ophelia stiffened in fear, then realized how silly it was. On her hand was Hamish's ring. She'd been unwilling to acknowledge the depth of her feelings, but could she bear to imagine her days without him? She'd found love and that love had been reciprocated. What was there to gain from being afraid?

She pressed herself into him, resting her hand upon his chest, and felt more at ease than she had in weeks. This was what she'd been searching for.

Enid and the Colonel declared their vows, to love each other through all difficulties, and to support one another, through joy and sorrow, sickness and health. Throughout, Hamish held Ophelia tightly.

'Are we thinking the same thing?' he whispered, his mouth against the crown of her head.

In response, she lifted his hand and pressed it to her cheek.

As the groom leaned in to give the bride her first kiss as the new Mrs Faversham, Hamish also turned to his love, his lips seeking out Ophelia's.

GIFTS

TOWARDS NOON, CHRISTMAS DAY, 1928

OPHELIA STAMPED her feet in the snow, as Horatio took his last few shots of the happy couple. "Do hurry up!' she hissed 'We're turning into icicles! I can see frost in the Colonel's moustache.'

Almost everyone else had made a beeline for the castle, as soon as the main group photograph had been taken. Hot mulled wine and mince pies awaited, and Morag had persuaded a couple of the estate workers to play the fiddle and pipes for entertainment.

'Thank you, my dear,' whispered Enid, as Ophelia walked behind with Marjorie, helping lift her veil. 'I hadn't realized it would take Mr Buffington so long to arrange us.'

'We'll soon have you warmed up,' Ophelia promised.

There was a rousing cheer as the newlyweds entered the Great Hall, where Morag had organized several of the party to create a sabre arch.

'Do be careful,' she'd urged, as the weapons were brought down from the wall. 'Hector likes to keep them sharp, in case of intruders!'

They soon moved through to the ballroom, where a great many circular tables had been set up, festooned with holly, poinsettias and white roses, upon crimson cloths, while silver bells and stars hung from the chandeliers. With windows floor to ceiling, and huge glass doors leading out onto the terrace, the room was the brightest in the castle. However, candelabras had been placed all about, ready to be lit as the afternoon light faded.

Through the centre of the room, a large space had been set aside for dancing.

'Splendid looking fare!' remarked Lady Faucett-Plumbley, eyeing the long table along one side of the room. All manner of birds and fish filled the platters. There was trout mousseline, and pheasant pâté, a selection of cold ham, chicken and venison, three sorts of game pie, poached salmon, hot buttered potatoes and caramelized onions, and a variety of pickles, not to mention Mrs Beesby's individual bannocks.

McFinn and Haddock whipped about with champagne, while the guests took their seats.

'Welcome everyone,' Morag announced. 'What a pleasure to see you here, at Castle Kintochlochie, and what a delight it is to celebrate with our dear friends, Enid and Montague. Let's raise our glasses to them, as they embark on their new adventures together.'

There was a hubbub of good wishes and the chink of flutes. The Colonel rose to make his own speech, ending with a kiss for his bride that would not have been amiss in one of Enid's novels. Morag then declared luncheon served and there was a dash for the buffet.

'Goodness me, mother,' remarked Daphne, taking Lady Morag by the arm. 'It's enough that you ask Mrs Beesby to act as both housekeeper and cook, but to serve this picnic arrangement, rather than a plated meal! It's too vulgar! People will think you can't afford to employ a full complement of staff.'

'The staff deserve some time to themselves on Christmas Day, Daphne,' Morag reasoned. 'This way, they can sit down to their own meal in peace. As for Mrs Beesby, she's really most efficient. There are only a handful of us living here most of the time. Constance and I pitch in to make sure things get done, and Ophelia has been splendid in helping Hamish make plans for the estate. She's such a clever girl. She's been reading up on all the latest techniques with livestock.'

'Knowing one end of a sheep from another is hardly likely to help her find a husband though, is it?' Lady Daphne sighed in exasperation. 'At least, not one of the right class.'

'I'm sure I didn't raise you to have such snobbish attitudes, Daphne.' Lady Morag turned a severe eye upon her daughter. 'You chose Peter without a title; he was only knighted for his business achievements some years after you were married, and had no political career at all when you met.'

'But I saw his potential!' argued Daphne. 'His family is among the wealthiest in Norfolk, and I could see he was driven.'

She looked over at Ophelia, whose head was bent close to that of Hamish. His hand, she would swear, was upon her daughter's lower back.

She felt a flush of anger. 'I can see that I was wrong to leave Ophelia in your hands, Mother. You've let her run rings around you. She clearly lacks the acuity to choose for herself, so it falls to us to guide her. Rather than doing so, you've allowed her to become over-familiar with those beneath her.'

'If you're referring to Hamish,' interjected Lady Morag, seeing the direction of her daughter's gaze, 'He is Lady Devonly's nephew. His father was well-educated and much respected in Aberdeenshire, while his mother, Constance's sister, was everything a well-bred woman should be.'

'But was she a 'Lady' in title, as well as bearing?' asked Daphne.

Morag pursed her lips. 'Constance's title hails from her

marriage to Lord Devonly, lately of His Majesty's Diplomatic Service. Her own family lacked any rank of nobility.'

'There we are then!' asserted Daphne. 'Ophelia is granddaughter to an earl, and I insist on nothing less for her.'

~

'Hamish has sloped off most mysteriously,' commented Ophelia, returning from her second run at the poached salmon. Her eyes flicked about the room, locating Felicité, and assuring herself that Hamish was nowhere near.

'A little bird tells me that he's been persuaded into a bit of play-acting.' Horatio smirked. 'At least he won't have to put on a beard for the role.'

From the hallway, there was the jingle of sleigh bells.

'Quiet, everyone,' Morag proclaimed. 'I invited another guest today, and I think his reindeer have just landed on the roof.'

There were several titters and an expectant hush fell as Hamish walked in, head to foot in red velvet. His middle had been well-padded with cushions, with a wide leather belt wrapped about the circumference. Over his shoulder, he carried a bulging bag, with another dragged behind.

'Now I understand why Granny wouldn't let us open our remaining gifts after breakfast! They must be in those sacks!' Ophelia whispered. 'Mind you, I've already had most of mine. Daddy slipped me a cheque this morning, and Mummy had wrapped five sets of thermal underwear.'

'Most practical,' commented Horatio. 'I nearly chose you the same myself.'

Ophelia giggled.

'Constance bought me a gorgeous cashmere shawl, and Granny gave me something too: a lovely pearl necklace from her own box. I'll wear it tomorrow, with my fawn dress.'

Hamish proceeded about the room, distributing parcels. Enid had wrapped signed copies of her books for every guest.

'How thrilling!' remarked Horatio, unveiling a copy of *Seduction on the South Seas.*

'That one's filled with desperate pirates,' explained Ophelia. 'I think Hector might have the same!' Even from several tables away, she could see his eyebrows twitching in suppressed disgust. Her own was entitled *Promised to the Marquess.*

'How apt!' said Horatio. 'There's something from me, too. I was up 'till all hours developing the photograph I took of everyone standing around the tree. Rather a nice keepsake, I thought.'

'How thoughtful you are!' Ophelia gave Horatio a kiss. 'I made some fudge with Mrs Beesby that's probably in Hamish's sack. Granny suggested I make lots, for all the guests to take home.'

She reached into her clutch bag and pulled out a box for Horatio. 'I was going to give this to you later, but you might as well have it now. Nothing much, of course; I have to make Daddy's cheques stretch quite a long way. I ordered it from an advert in *The Lady* last month: ranked eighth in the 'top ten gifts for the man in your life', apparently.'

There was a small globe, with a likeness of a Cairn terrier inside, against a background of mountains. Horatio gave it a shake and 'snow' drifted all about. 'Just like Pudding, I thought,' said Ophelia. 'I've bought the same for Hamish, with a wolfhound inside, and one for the Colonel with a labrador, and one for Granny with a Pekinese. It's a shame that everyone doesn't have a dog. I'd have been able to get all my shopping done in one swoop. The rest have had to make do with a bar of Penhaligon's soap.'

'Genius, darling! No one would give me such a present but you!'

'Crikey!' exclaimed Marjorie, hurrying over to join them. 'I hadn't expected my offerings to be pulled out of a sack. I've knitted you all mittens, but some are rather better than others. I was finishing off the last of them on the drive up and the road was jolly bumpy.'

'I'm sure they'll go down a treat,' Ophelia assured her. 'I could do with some new ones.' From across the room, she could see the Colonel pulling a striped jumper out of some tissue paper; one sleeve looked considerably longer than the other.

'I had to make him something special, being my new brother-in-law,' Marjorie admitted. 'I hope you won't mind just having the mittens. I didn't have enough wool to make everyone a pullover.'

With a farewell wave, Father Christmas departed, and McFinn and Haddock reappeared, setting about lighting the many candles. It was barely two in the afternoon, but dusk was already approaching.

The maids cleared the savoury dishes and, at last, Mrs Beesby entered with a huge Christmas Pudding on a silver tray. Haddock stepped forward to douse the heavy fruit cake with brandy and struck a match. There was a collective gasp as the alcohol lit and the pudding was engulfed in blue flames.

'My favourite!' said Ophelia, rubbing her hands. 'I hope there's plenty of brandy butter to go with it.'

A variety of other desserts also appeared: blancmanges and jellies, and individual bowls of cranachan, bursting with whisky-soaked raspberries and whipped cream, honey, and toasted oats. For each table, there were bowls of dates stuffed with marzipan, and chocolate covered nuts, as well as coffee liqueurs.

It hardly seemed possible that anyone would be able to dance after eating so much but Enid and the Colonel led the way, taking the floor to the accompaniment of the fiddle and pipe playing *Marry Me Now*. As several other couples rose to join them, the instruments took up the lively melody of *Mairi's Wedding*.

Morag then organized everyone in some traditional Ceilidh dancing, launching with an *Eightsome Reel* and then straight into a frenetic attempt at *Strip the Willow*. Several guests were learning as they went and getting in rather a muddle.

Ophelia had managed a brief spin with Hamish, who'd changed back into his formal kilt dress, and was drawing many admiring glances.

'I must sit down,' she gasped. 'I've the most awful stitch. My own fault for eating a spoonful of all the puddings. You keep going, darling.'

Ophelia was only half-way across the room when Felicité appeared at her side, leading someone Ophelia had been at pains to avoid.

'You know Mr Belton, my knight in shining armour, who rescued us from our punctured tyre? Did he not take you for a spin in his car, Ophelia, in the summer?' Felicité rested her hand proprietorially upon his shoulder and looked at Ophelia with a certain wickedness.

'Mr Belton is all modesty, and wouldn't tell me just how well-acquainted you are but, by his blushes, I may perhaps guess.'

'Really Felicité, your imagination is wasted in acting. You ought to be writing the scripts,' retorted Ophelia, though her own remembrance of that day in Peregrine's motor brought some redness to her cheek.

'You did pick rather a ghastly place to break down, Mrs Worthington,' said the young man in question, clearly deciding that discretion was the better part of valour and that the least said of his relations with Ophelia the better.

'That particular public house is frequented by estate workers and local farming hands. Good chaps, obviously, but mostly related to one another in ways frowned upon by the Old Testament.'

Peregrine laughed at his own joke. 'One fellow was in the midst of giving the other a jolly good biff on the nose and the rest looked likely to join in at any moment. I feared we'd stumbled upon some ancient Celtic blood feud.'

'It was all most arousing.' Felicité's lips curled in remembrance.

'There is something, is there not, about men with dirt beneath the nails?'

'I'm sure you understand me, Ophelia,' she said, inclining her head towards Hamish, who was currently partnering Lady Faucett-Plumbley for *The Dashing White Sergeant*.

Felicité selected a chocolate from a nearby table and bit into it with relish, letting her long, crimson nail linger at her lips, allowing the candlelight to catch the facets of the huge diamond upon her finger.

'*À bientôt.*' Felicité fluttered her lashes and glided away, steering Peregrine before her.

Pure jealousy, thought Ophelia, and congratulated herself on having remained civil. Only another day or so, and the dreadful Mrs Worthington would surely be gone.

PEREGRINE'S PROPOSAL

LATE AFTERNOON, CHRISTMAS DAY, 1928

DECIDING that the musicians deserved a well-earned rest, Hamish put on the gramophone and came to find Ophelia, leading her out for a Foxtrot. Sir Peter and Lady Daphne whisked past them, Ophelia's father smiling amiably, though her mother's face was stony.

Hamish ended the dance by dipping Ophelia to the floor and giving her a kiss.

'My goodness, you're amorous today!' she laughed. It was wonderful for Hamish to show his affection for her publicly, but she knew it would generate a lot of talk. It could only be a matter of time before her mother intervened.

Hamish nuzzled her neck. 'I want everyone to see how much I love you.' He lifted her hand to his lips: the hand upon which she was wearing his ring.

'May I step in?' came a voice to one side. It was Flavia, the Faucett-Plumbley's granddaughter. 'You two are obviously an item, so I don't want to be a pill, but there are so few young men here. I don't think I can bear another turn around the room with someone old enough to be my grandfather.'

'Of course,' smiled Ophelia. 'You have my blessing to borrow him.'

Ophelia's father, Sir Peter, was next to sweep her across the floor, followed by Horatio. After several dances, Ophelia begged for a chance to rest her feet, and have a cup of reviving fruit punch.

'What a whizz you are!' Ophelia fell exhausted into a nearby chair. 'Your Sugar Step is even better than your Charleston, Horatio. Where did you learn to be so light on your feet?'

'I'm endeavouring to have a misspent youth, and putting in all the hours required.' Horatio, eyeing the fruit punch with suspicion, swiped two flutes of champagne from a passing tray. 'I know all the best clubs, in Paris now, as well as in London: the ones that turn a blind eye, regardless of how outrageous their guests become. The stories I could tell you!' He took a sip from his glass. 'But you're far too innocent. I won't be the one to corrupt you.'

Ophelia gave him an admonishing smack.

'You are made for country air and wholesome men, like our delicious Hamish,' said Horatio. 'And where is that lovely man? It should be him twirling you into hysterics, not me.'

'Good question,' said Ophelia. 'He was dancing with Constance a while ago, and then granny, until Enid demanded a Tango. I'd no idea that Hamish could dance but, apparently, Felicité taught him...'

Horatio raised his brows in mock-horror. 'Speak not the devil's name, for she will appear!'

Ophelia sighed. 'I'm trying to be a grown-up about it all. Hardly Hamish's fault that she got her claws into him. She's toxic, but men lose all sense when she's around. I'm attempting to turn the other cheek.'

'You're a saint,' proclaimed Horatio, passing her the second flute.

With a clap of her hands, Morag drew everyone's attention again, and called for a short break, so that those who wished to might change into evening attire. Almost all were staying the night, and therefore had bedrooms to repair to.

Hamish, of course, was already changed. Looking about the room, Ophelia saw him with Hector. Hamish was so patient. No matter how demanding Hector became, Hamish always had time for him, and was adept at calming the old man's temper.

She would race up to put on her long gown and then grab Hamish on her return, for more dancing. Why not let everyone see them together! She was free, wasn't she, to decide who to love? Lady Morag would plead Ophelia's case with her parents, if that was required.

It seemed an age since that morning, when she and Hamish had been in the stables together. Could one's feelings grow so much stronger in a single day? Perhaps she was just swept up in the romanticism of the occasion.

Crossing the hall, she decided to look in on the dogs, who were closeted in Hector's study, out of the way of their guests. Four wagging tails greeted her, with Pudding pushing to the front, to claim her mistress' first attention.

After receiving a quick pat down his back, Rex, the Colonel's labrador, slunk back to take prime spot in front of the fire, with Hamish's wolfhound, Braveheart, curling beside him. Aphrodite gave Ophelia's hand a lick, before returning to where she'd been sleeping, in Hector's armchair. Pudding sat on Ophelia's foot, looking up with baleful eyes, as if they'd been parted for days rather than only a few hours.

'Come on then, my little Pudding,' said Ophelia, picking the terrier up for a cuddle. 'Let's go to the window and see how deep the snow has gotten.'

She felt a slight chill pass over her, looking out, just as she and

Horatio had done only the night before. The light was fading quickly, taking on a violet hue, the sun low in the sky beyond the mountains. Her thoughts returned to the strange figure who'd partially strangled her. The bruising was slight enough to be covered by face powder, but her neck was still tender.

Ophelia heard the click of the door opening and turned in alarm, suddenly fearing that her assailant had returned.

It was only Peregrine, however. Newly changed into his evening suit, he'd oiled down his dark curls, to make them sit flat across his head. The dogs looked over, but didn't bother to shift themselves.

'I've been wanting to talk to you,' Peregrine began. His eyes darted nervously about the room, as if to check they truly were alone. 'I've been thinking about what happened, in the summer...' He coughed and stepped closer.

'There's really no need to talk about that,' said Ophelia, wondering how best to extricate herself. Might she just walk past him and leave? Or would it be too impolite?

'I'm a man of the world now and I realize that my actions were over-hasty,' said Peregrine, placing his hand upon Ophelia's arm.

Her eyes narrowed. Ophelia remembered all too well the outing in Peregrine's car.

'I can see now that you're a modern gal, and that I shouldn't have judged so harshly.' Peregrine leaned in, his lips brushing Ophelia's hair. 'Can't we give it another go, old bean?'

'Mr Belton!' snapped Ophelia, moving away from the window, and around to the other side of the sofa, depositing Pudding on a cushion. 'I think you've had one glass of fizz too many.'

'Perhaps I have,' he admitted, 'But it's only making me bold enough to say what I really feel.' He followed her, reaching for Ophelia's arm once more. 'Mrs Worthington — Felicité — has shown me that it's dashed silly to wait until we're married before enjoying ourselves.'

'I'm sure that Mrs Worthington has shown you all sorts of things,' answered Ophelia huffily. 'As for me, I'm spoken for!'

Peregrine looked pointedly at Ophelia's engagement finger.

'Are you sure, old thing?' He lifted her hand to his cheek. 'I understand you being cross with me, of course, but I'd worship the dance floor under your slippered feet. I'd take you to the moon and back! I'd even let you have a go behind the wheel of my motor... just for a little while.'

'It's a marvellous offer Peregrine,' said Ophelia, gritting her teeth and attempting to pull away, 'But I'll have to decline.'

Pudding, deciding that her mistress was in need of a helping hand, launched herself from the cushions, jumping over the back of the sofa to land a juicy bite on Peregrine's left buttock. Her jaws closed at the optimum moment, giving her a generous mouthful of trouser.

With a shriek, Peregrine unhanded Ophelia.

'Dogs are such loyal companions,' she commented, darting round to scoop the terrier from where she was dangling. 'And such excellent instincts when it comes to character!'

Leaving Peregrine cursing, Ophelia departed the room.

'That was very naughty, Pudding,' she whispered in the terrier's furry little ear. 'But also jolly athletic, and well-judged, as it happens.'

She gave the twitching nose both a gentle tap and a kiss. 'Now, I really must put on my evening gown, find Hamish and get him on the dancefloor.'

LADY DAPHNE INTERVENES

EARLY EVENING, CHRISTMAS DAY, 1928

As soon as she entered her bedroom, Ophelia had the feeling that someone had been there in her absence. Uneasily, she went to the dressing table. Nothing was missing, and her clothes had not been moved, or damaged. Mary, Lady Morag's maid, had removed the green silk dress and all else was as it should be.

And yet...

Ophelia shivered and drew down her red velvet gown from its place in the wardrobe. With black beading at the shoulders and hem, and a rather low cut back, it was a sophisticated dress that she hadn't worn a great deal. She felt rather a fraud in such clothes. They were for women who knew themselves, and Ophelia couldn't help the notion that she was still searching for whoever she wanted to be.

The gown suited her though. A slick of matching red lipstick and another coat of mascara and she felt very pleased with her appearance. Looking in the mirror, her eyes shone back, large and dark.

She passed her brush through her hair and fastened her diamond clip to the side. Yes, she'd do! She could show Hamish that she was just as alluring as his former flame.

Enough! thought Ophelia. I'm spending far too much energy comparing myself to that awful person! Hamish loves me for being me.

'Stand guard for me, Pudding,' she said, leaving the Cairn sitting on the bed. 'Don't let anyone come in here whilst I'm gone, even if they offer you a plate of ham and pickles!'

Pudding looked up at her mistress forlornly. Abandoned again! At least this time she'd have Ophelia's pillow to put her head upon.

∽

Ophelia had just passed her mother's room when she heard Lady Daphne's voice behind her.

'We have something to discuss, Ophelia,' she called after her. 'Come in here, if you please.'

It was not a tone which would brook dissent.

Lady Daphne was wearing a slender sheath dress in black crepe. On anyone else, it would have been too sombre, especially for a wedding, the only adornment being some orchids embroidered into the hip in silver thread. On Ophelia's mother, the dress was simply chic.

'How cold these rooms are,' said Lady Daphne, tilting her head to fasten diamond-drop earrings. 'I keep thinking someone has left a window open.'

'No, Mummy. It's just the draughts up here. You must remember?'

'I do my best to forget what's unpleasant to me. There's only one thing I cannot forget and that is your unmarried state.'

Ophelia scowled, which her mother pointedly ignored.

Opening her jewel box, Lady Daphne took out a choker, studded with brilliants, holding it to her neck and bending at the knee, that her daughter might secure the clasp.

'Beauty does not endure,' she continued. 'Even blessed with my genes, you'll find that you have a small window of opportunity where a husband is concerned. You must adopt the right attitude, Ophelia.'

Rising to her full height, she turned and looked down on her daughter, her tone imperious.

'Your father and I leave for Achnagarry Castle the day after tomorrow, to see in the New Year with the Camerons, but we'll collect you on our return, and take you back to London with us.'

Ophelia reached over to the bedpost to steady herself, lowering to sit on the coverlet.

'I doubt that Percival will still consider you. His father died last month, leaving him to succeed to the title. He's become exceptionally popular, with three of the King's grand-nieces expressing interest. I've no idea how you allowed him to slip through your fingers.' Lady Daphne sighed heavily.

'However, we may yet be able to find someone suitable. You won't mind, I suppose, if they have some small foible? The young Marquess of Frittlington is known to be a little too fond of the housemaids but he's avoided his father's predilection for gambling, and I hear his twitch is much improved since he gave up attending social events. His mother, with whom I have cultivated an acquaintance, agrees that a quiet girl, happy to stay at home, would suit him.'

Ophelia raised her head.

'There is someone I'm quite keen on,' she began. 'I still don't know if I'm ready to be married yet but, if I do, I'd like it to be him who asks.'

'Well, that's more of the right attitude,' replied Lady Daphne. 'Has my mother managed to introduce you to someone useful while you've been here? I had no expectations, but anything is possible, I suppose.'

Ophelia balled her fists, willing herself to be brave.

'It's Hamish, Mummy, who manages the estate. He's Lady Devonly's nephew. His father was only an engineer but quite a famous one. He helped build the Forth Bridge.'

'Don't be ridiculous, Ophelia.' Lady Daphne stepped closer, her eyes glaring. 'I don't care if his father built the royal residence of Sandringham single-handed. He's simply not our class. Besides which, he's employed by your grandmother. It's just not done, Ophelia. You might as well throw your lot in with the stable boy!'

'I'm not listening anymore,' declared Ophelia, rising to her feet. 'I've been happier at Kintochlochie than I ever was in London. I'm going to stay with Granny and help her run the estate.' She strode boldly to the door. 'This is my home now, with people who truly care about me!'

Fighting back her tears, she stepped into the corridor, pulling the door shut behind her.

FIT TO DROP

EARLY EVENING, CHRISTMAS DAY, 1928

'Some holiday! grumbled Gertie. 'My feet are ready to fall off with going up and down them stairs today, carrying endless plates of food. I don't know where they're putting it!'

'It's the glassware what does for me,' added Bessie. 'All that drying and polishing!'

'Mrs B's dinner was right tasty though, weren't it?' Gladys rubbed her stomach appreciatively.

'Bit rich for me,' sniffed Gertie, replacing silver cutlery in its box, ready to go into the safe. 'And those sprouts are repeating themselves something rotten.'

'And it's me what's got to share a room with you!' said Bessie, clicking her tongue.

'You didn't eat much, Hettie. You feeling alright?' asked Gladys. 'I've been meaning to say I hope there's no hard feelings, what with me and Murray stepping out.'

Hettie looked up from the basket of napkins she was carrying through to the laundry room and frowned in confusion.

'In a world of her own, as usual,' murmured Gertie.

'Just tired,' said Hettie. 'It's that camp bed, like Gladys were saying, keeping me from my sleep.'

Mrs Beesby bustled in from the pantry, carrying another two trays of petit fours. 'Good job we made extras! They're wolfing those Florentines like there's no tomorrow.'

Her eyes alighted on Hettie, heaving the dirty napkins onwards.

'Goodness me, Hettie! You look fit to drop. I hope you haven't caught Ethel's flu.'

She took the basket from Hettie, setting it on the floor, and placed her hand on the young girl's forehead.

'No fever, but better safe than sorry. Up to your room, now, and straight to bed. Stay there in the morning too, and we'll send up a tray. If you're no better, we'll get the doctor to look at you.'

'You're very kind, Mrs Beesby.'

'You're one of my girls, aren't you? Who'll look after you if not me? We all answer for our sins in the end, but I'd rather stand at the Pearly Gates knowing I've done more good than harm.'

Hettie gave a little sob.

'Over-tired is what you are.' Mrs Beesby shook her head and went to the lower drawer of the dresser. 'Take this, Hettie; one of my sleeping powders. You need rest more than anything, I'd say.'

Hettie nodded her head and slipped the packet into her pocket.

SEDUCTION

MID-EVENING, CHRISTMAS DAY, 1928

HAMISH GLANCED AGAIN at his watch. Almost an hour had passed since he'd seen Ophelia leave, at Morag's suggestion that guests might change into their evening attire. The ballroom had become full again, and was rowdier than ever.

He stifled a yawn. Having barely slept the night before, he was ready to turn in, but he knew Ophelia would want to dance, when she reappeared. Meanwhile, he might take a breather in the library — get away from the hubbub for a few minutes.

The room was blessedly quiet, and in darkness save for a single lamp. The fire had almost gone out, but there was enough life in the embers to coax a flame. He settled himself in the armchair nearest the hearth and closed his eyes.

Just ten minutes, he thought, then I'll go looking for Ophelia.

~

He was roused by the tickle of slender fingers reaching beneath his kilt, two hands, moving upwards, stroking the hair on his thighs.

'Ophelia?' he murmured. His eyes, having closed, were reluctant to open.

'*C'est moi, chéri,*' came a soft voice, the owner of which lowered her lips to kiss Hamish's bare knee.

He jerked awake, to see Felicité sitting on the floor at his feet.

'Great Gods! What are you doing?' Hamish pulled himself upright, and his knees together. He could take a pretty good guess where she'd been looking before she woke him and, thanks to her stroking of his leg, there had certainly been something to look at!

'Aren't you pleased to see me?' She lowered her chin, to look up at him through her lashes.

He recognized the dress Felicité was wearing as one she'd favoured back in the summer. It had been a difficult decision, to push away his feelings for Ophelia, and take Felicité to Edinburgh, but their relationship had been one of long-standing. He'd owed it to her to keep the promises he'd made. How hopeful he'd been, that they might make a go of it. Pure foolishness, he'd soon realized. Felicité was far too ambitious to remain with him in Scotland, and too self-centred to compromise. He also suspected that she'd been unfaithful to him, on more than one occasion, and with multiple lovers.

Of sheerest nude chiffon, her gown left little to the imagination; the silver beading barely covered the fullness of her breasts. As she shifted to sit up on her knees, her right nipple strained against the fabric, clearly visible.

When his wife had died, and the baby they'd so longed for, he'd thought he'd never escape from the grief. His relationship with Felicité had been a distraction, at least: had finally given him something to think about other than his loss. In the end, however, she'd only made things more complicated. Had Ophelia not been so forgiving, his chance of love with a woman who truly cared for him would have been dashed.

Felicité snaked her arms upwards, to his waist, pressing her breasts against his knee, her eyes half-closing.

'Do you remember, Hamish, how you used to punish me when I'd been wicked? You know I'm not wearing any under-things. My bottom is quite bare.'

Despite himself, Hamish felt a stirring in his groin.

'No one needs to know. It will be our secret. You can take me here if you like. I know you want to. Are you growing big for me?'

'That's enough,' said Hamish, pushing her away and standing up.

She rose to her feet also, almost as tall as he, in her heels. 'I mean no harm, Hamish,' she said softly. 'It's only that I miss you. It was always you that I loved, always you that I wanted…'

She walked over to the decanter and poured them both a whisky.

'I won't, if you don't mind,' said Hamish, placing his to one side. 'I've the livestock to check on before I go to bed tonight.'

'*Merveilleux!* I should like to see them.' She looked up at him, resting her hand upon his chest. 'Let's go to the barn together. Throw me in the straw and have your way with me. We've never made love in a barn before.'

'I don't think you've 'made love' anywhere, Felicité,' said Hamish, removing her fingers as she attempted to undo his buttons. 'You consume men like some ravenous mantis and spit the remains out afterwards.'

Felicité pouted. Not getting her own way always made her petulant.

'How do you think I felt, waking up to an empty hotel room and a note telling me that you were heading to America with Ranulph, to make some film?'

'Opportunities, darling!' Felicité angled herself, with obvious intent to give him the best view of her breasts. 'I could hardly say no. It's not every day that someone asks you to play Cleopatra.'

'I suppose not, but it's not every day that I ask a woman to marry me, either,' said Hamish, looking down at her with ill-concealed contempt.

'I noticed,' said Felicité, moving close. 'You haven't asked Ophelia; or if you have, she's declined?'

'It's none of your damned business,' said Hamish, grasping her by the wrist. 'And for God's sake, stop caressing my chest. You're a married woman. I may not have been wealthy enough to tempt you but someone clearly was. Behave with a bit of modesty.'

She drained one of the tumblers of whisky, then replaced it on the side-table.

'Why not come to Hollywood with me, darling? I'm filming *Marie Antoinette* and you might play one of my lovers. They would love you, *mon cher*. We would set the celluloid on fire. Your strong arms pinning your queen to the bed as you have your way.'

She smoothed the fabric of her dress, pulling it tight over her curves.

'I've no yearning to ponce about in front of a camera, Felicité. I would've thought you'd know me better than that.'

'As you wish.'

She picked up the second glass and emptied it. She had the face of an angel, with her fair hair and blue eyes, but the look she gave him was utterly devilish.

'Kiss me?' Felicité parted her lips and licked them, her pupils huge. 'Just once? For old time's sake?'

You can go to Hell!' said Hamish, attempting to push past her.

'I probably will, *mon chéri*, but I intend to have some fun before then.'

Her grasp upon his arm was sudden, jerking him towards her, taking him by surprise. Her face was raised to his before he had a chance to pull away. He found himself tempted to clasp her pliant body, and to kiss her hard. He'd show her what she'd thrown away.

His hand grasped the back of her head, and his mouth was almost upon hers, as the door opened.

BETRAYAL

9PM, CHRISTMAS DAY, 1928

IT TOOK some moments for Ophelia to find her voice, standing in the doorway to the library. The room was dimly lit but she could see clearly enough: Hamish's hand darting to the woman's bare back, almost ferocious in its motion, jolting her forward, and his other grabbing a handful of that distinctively silver blonde hair, twisting her head to one side, as he lowered his lips to meet hers.

No one else's hair was that particular hue. No one else would dare wear such a dress.

Ophelia felt the blood drain from her face, and then rush through again, in a fierce blaze of heat.

'Is she really so irresistible?' Ophelia's words rang out, clipped and vehement, unwavering despite the icy numbness travelling through her limbs.

Hamish's head shot up and Ophelia saw the lingering fury in his expression, mixed with something else: lust, she supposed. Recognizing Ophelia, Hamish's anger ebbed away, replaced by confusion, and then fear. He released his hold upon the woman in his arms.

He whispered Ophelia's name, but she made no move, nor replied.

Felicité looked over her shoulder, replacing the fallen strap of her dress slowly, allowing Ophelia the opportunity to view the exposed curve of her left breast.

'*Quel dommage*! Just as things were becoming interesting,' sighed Felicité. 'How tiresome it is to be interrupted.'

Turning, Ophelia walked away, across the marble floor of the Great Hall. Despite her wish to run, she controlled herself. She wouldn't allow Hamish, or Felicité, the pleasure of seeing how devastated she was; how, once again, the tempestuous love affair between them had dashed Ophelia's hopes. Her throat ached with the weeping she was determined to suppress and her eyes welled, leaving her feet to carry her blindly up the stairs. As she turned onto the landing corridor, she identified Mr Belton, absorbed in kissing a young woman she placed as the Faucett-Plumbley's granddaughter. A laugh rose in her, but emerged as a sob, and she stumbled onwards, falling into the wood panelling, almost toppling a lamp from a small table before reaching her room.

Only with the door safely closed behind her did she allow herself to wail, with hurt and indignation. She turned the key and then flung herself upon the bed. Pudding sent up her own howl of alarm at seeing her mistress so distressed.

Barely a minute passed before there was a knock at her door, and Hamish's voice, urging Ophelia to let him in, to allow him to speak to her, to explain.

Ophelia took a pillow and placed it over her head. She would pretend that she'd never met him, that he didn't exist.

The handle rattled, and Hamish persisted, but the door remained closed to him.

MALICIOUS INTENT

LATE EVENING, CHRISTMAS DAY, 1928

WHEN THERE WERE no more tears, Ophelia sat up. Hadn't she cried enough over Hamish, that summer? It was time to pull herself together. She'd had the truth brought home to her the hard way but, by God, she was determined that it make her wiser. It was naïve of her to have thought Hamish could resist what was being offered on a plate.

Well! Ophelia declared to herself. He can sicken himself on French tart all he likes!

In her distress, she'd thrown herself onto her bed, still wearing her shoes. Vehemently, she kicked them off, then flung her dress over her head, sending it into a heap on the floor, where Pudding gave it an investigatory sniff. It had been a long evening, and the terrier's eyes were closing as she nestled onto the folds of fabric.

Ophelia donned her fleeced robe, pulling the knot tight at her waist, then sat at the dressing table. Her eyes, red-rimmed, felt as if they'd had salt rubbed into them.

What a sight you look! Ophelia chided herself. And all for a man!

She snapped her jewellery from her ears, dropping it into her trinket box, followed by the hair clip. As she removed the ring Hamish had given her that morning, she fought down a wave of sadness. There was no point in indulging those sorts of feelings. She'd been a fool. That was all.

Ophelia found that she was wide awake and she didn't relish the idea of lying brooding for hours. I'll have a bath to soothe me, she thought. Gathering her sponge bag and the lamp from beside her bed, she ventured out. Funds hadn't yet permitted the extension of electric lighting upstairs, so it was terribly dark

The bathroom wasn't far, but the corridor seemed to stretch on, disappearing into blackness. From down below, elsewhere in the castle, sounds of merrymaking drifted up to her: people dancing, drinking and laughing. Here, the silence prickled at her shoulders. She felt quite alone.

She'd almost reached the bathroom when something brushed her arm, making her jump, but it was only one of the tapestries on the wall, billowing out in the draught. Since the unpleasant experience in Hector's study, and with her dress, she didn't feel at ease in the castle; as if something, or someone, had malicious intent towards her.

Ophelia was about to turn the doorknob to the bathroom, when the door swept open. A shriek caught in her throat as a face appeared.

'Good Heavens, Ophelia!' came a familiar voice. 'You made me start!' Lady Daphne raised her own lamp. 'For a moment, I imagined something perfectly silly. In that pale blue dressing gown, you rather resembled the figure I saw the other night, in our bedroom. I don't know what's gotten into me lately. I'm not usually so ridiculous.'

'Mummy!' cried Ophelia, and clasped herself to Lady Daphne, also attired in her dressing gown.

Her mother patted her back. 'There, there. Has this dark corridor made you nervous, too? There's no one here but us. Everyone's still enjoying the party. I had one of my heads coming on, so decided to call it a night.'

Ophelia had never been so pleased to see her mother.

'I've made a decision,' she said on impulse. 'I'll join you, when you return from Achnagarry Castle, and I'll go back to London for a while.' She bit her lip. 'I need a break from Kintochlochie... at least for some time...'

'Splendid!' said Lady Daphne, stepping into the corridor. 'I knew you'd see sense.'

❧

Ophelia placed her lantern on the floor and sank into the warm water, submerging her shoulders. Closing her eyes, she endeavoured to ignore the dripping of the tap, and clear her mind.

She felt wretched. Unable to help herself, she imagined Hamish already in Felicité's bed; or perhaps he'd bring her to his own, no matter that the sheets still bore the perfume of Ophelia's body.

She'd long known that Felicité was unscrupulous when it came to pursuing men, but she'd believed Hamish was hers now: that he'd be able to control any lingering desire for his former lover.

Damn! thought Ophelia. Damn! Damn! Damn!

She kept her eyes closed, concentrating on those things which had brought her happiness: the beauty of the mountains, the way that sunlight played through the forest, the wonderful horse rides she'd taken around the estate, and the simple pleasure of taking Pudding for a walk around the loch.

Her thoughts turned to her grandmother. It had been wonderful to get to know Lady Morag; she'd been so generous, and supportive of Ophelia's desire to make more of herself, to be more than just someone's wife. She'd seen her talents and encouraged them, rather than thinking she was good only for finding a husband. She'd miss Morag, and Constance, too.

Ophelia opened her eyes and shivered; the water had begun to turn cold. She realized then how little she could see, the room being lit only by a sliver of moonlight from the window. Her lamp, it appeared, had gone out.

There was a slight shuffling sound from the far side of the room, where the shadows hung thick. The bathroom had been converted from one of the smaller bedrooms; one wall remained wood-panelled in dark oak, although the rest had been tiled. Was there a mouse in the room, or a rat? She wished she'd brought Pudding.

Perhaps the dark had disoriented her, and the movement was on the other side of the door. Someone might be out there, waiting to come in. She'd locked the door, hadn't she? It would be rather embarrassing to have Hector or the Colonel suddenly poke their head in.

'Hello,' Ophelia called. 'Is someone there?'

Her voice echoed off the cold tiles.

Ophelia leaned forward, reaching for her towel. As she did so, she saw a pale figure rise from the corner, all in white, its head lowered beneath its hood.

Her scream surprised even herself, so loudly did it ring out. The figure stooped to snatch Ophelia's dressing gown and then whisked away, back to the darkest corner of the room.

It was all over in moments, but Ophelia found she could hardly breathe, as if the shock of what she'd seen had knocked the breath from her body. Truly, the castle had a ghost; one that could pass through locked doors to terrorize its victims. Had her screams not driven it away, would it have placed its hands about her neck again? Did it wish not only to frighten her, but to take her to join it on the other side?

Ophelia rose from the water, shivering in fright, her fingers fumbling for the towel. She had placed but one foot on the cold floor when she heard heavy footsteps in the corridor; those of someone running. In haste, she swung her other leg over the edge of the bath, and found her heel skidding from under her. She landed heavily, hitting her hip and the side of her knee.

Her eyes smarted with the pain and she let out a sob.

Someone rattled at the door and Ophelia felt her heart constrict in fear, but it was Hamish's voice she heard.

'Is that you, Ophelia?'

He shook the handle again.

'Answer me, or I'll kick this door in!'

'I'm alright,' said Ophelia, but her voice had shrunk to nothing.

'I'm coming in,' declared Hamish. 'If you're near the door, try to move back.'

A few moments later, the door flew open, and Hamish was there, still dressed in his formal evening attire, his jacket and kilt. Dropping to his knees, he rolled her onto her back, with the towel covering her, then scooped beneath her shoulders and knees to lift her into his arms.

He carried her swiftly from the room, back to her own, placing her carefully upon the coverlet, where Ophelia lay quite still. Looking up at Hamish, several emotions fought within her, yet she seemed unable to say a word, her mouth opening without sound emerging.

'You're in shock, Ophelia,' said Hamish. 'Don't try to speak.' He eased her body beneath the covers, tucking them firmly around her. 'Thank God I heard you. I mightn't have if I'd been in my room, but I'd just come back from checking on the animals. Your scream carried down the corridor.'

He surveyed her closely, pressing his fingers to her wrist. 'We need to get you warmed up, and something hot and sweet would be a good idea. I'll go downstairs and bring back some cocoa.'

He rose to go and the thought terrified her. 'No!' she cried. She swallowed hard, willing the words to shape in her mouth. 'It might come back.'

Hamish sat down at once. 'What might come back, Ophelia? What happened?'

She shook her head, unable to articulate her fears.

'I won't be long. I'll lock the door behind me, and take the key. You'll be safe from whatever's frightened you, Ophelia.' He looked down at her with tender concern.

'Don't go,' she said again, her eyes pleading.

He touched her cheek, brushing her hair from her face. 'You truly want me to stay?'

She nodded.

'Then I won't go anywhere, and I won't let anything hurt you, Ophelia.'

Without removing his jacket, he lay on the coverlet, rubbing her back to warm her.

By the time he whispered 'I love you', Ophelia had already fallen asleep.

∿

The morning light was coming dimly through the windows when Ophelia woke, the curtains having been drawn back. She shifted to sit up, then winced, as her hip reminded her of all that had happened the night before.

'I've brought you a tray,' said Hamish, setting it on her lap. She looked down at the two soft-boiled eggs and toast soldiers, and the tea brewing in its pot. Normally, she'd have fallen on it with delight but, this morning, she had no appetite. The toast had been thickly buttered and the thought of putting it in her mouth made her feel slightly sick.

Hamish sat on the edge of the bed, still wearing his clothes of the night before. He'd never appeared more tired, his eyes dark-shadowed. His complexion looked almost grey.

Part of her wanted to rage at him, to pick up both eggs and throw them at the wall, to toss the tray in the air and scream, but

Ophelia was weary, too. She'd spent most of her anger in tears, and was left with a terrible hollow in her chest.

There was something else troubling her besides her remembrance of Hamish's faithlessness. The strange figure, looming from the darkness, had disappeared just as quickly. She'd been so frightened, and Hamish had found her, and brought her back to her own bed. Had he stayed with her all night?

'Try to eat something, Ophelia.' Hamish poured tea into the cup. 'You saw something that upset you, but it wasn't at all what you think.'

She frowned. 'It was a ghost, Hamish. It can't have been anything else. The way it came into the bathroom … and then vanished. You know the door was locked. I'm not imagining things.'

Hamish looked perplexed. 'You must have fallen asleep, and the shadows played tricks on you. Then you woke in a panic, slipped and fell. I came when I heard your shriek.' He reached for her arm, lowering his eyes. 'But that wasn't what I meant. You saw something else, in the library.'

'I've not forgotten,' said Ophelia, moving her arm away. She didn't want to be touched by him. 'I thought you'd have more sense than to be infected by her poison a second time.'

Hamish sighed heavily. 'I'm no fool, Ophelia.'

She pushed the tray to one side and eased her legs from the bed. 'You weren't making sufficient efforts to discourage her,' she retorted. 'I gave you the benefit of the doubt when you were stuck in the cupboard together, but I'd be an idiot to ignore the fact that you'd have kissed her if I hadn't interrupted you last night.'

'You're right,' he admitted, running his hands through his hair. 'I tried to leave before things got out of hand but Felicité is adept at provocation. God help me! I should know better by now…' He rose, walking round the bed to face Ophelia. 'Believe me, nothing of consequence happened.'

'Well!' hissed Ophelia, her eyes suddenly blazing. 'Let's give you a medal for your restraint, shall we? Far be it from me to interfere with the natural urges of a red-blooded male.'

Hamish flinched but said nothing.

Ophelia pushed her feet into her slippers and reached for her dressing gown, hanging over the back of a chair.

'I don't want to lose my temper with you, Hamish.' She made herself look him in the face. 'We've meant so much to each other.'

He stepped forward, hopefully, reaching for Ophelia's arm again, but she shook her head.

'I've told my mother that I'll spend some time with her, in London.'

'But you'll come back?' said Hamish, a wild desperation entering his eyes. 'Promise me you'll come back, Ophelia.'

'I can't say... I don't know.' Ophelia turned away. 'It's best for you to go now, Hamish.'

~

Ophelia stood for some time, looking out the window at the snow-covered landscape. She was determined not to cry further tears. Better for her to know where she stood, and make an informed decision about her future. The thought of returning to London with her mother filled her with little joy but it would give her time to think. She might forgive Hamish, but could she trust him?

She should get dressed, she supposed. Enid and the Colonel were heading off today, on their honeymoon. She wanted to be ready in time to say farewell. Turning again to face the room, Ophelia couldn't help feeling that something was amiss.

Pudding was still lying on her evening dress, heaped where she'd discarded it the night before. Ophelia knelt down and gave the little dog a shake, which produced the desired outcome. Pudding yawned sleepily and wagged her tail.

'What a long doze you've had, Pudding. Not like you at all!' said Ophelia, picking the terrier up for a cuddle.

With a surge of panic, Ophelia realized what had been worrying her. The dressing gown she'd put on was the very one she'd worn to the bathroom, and which had been whisked away by the pale hand of the strange figure. How had it returned to her room, when the door had been locked all night? She shuddered at the thought, wrenching the robe open, and dropping it to the floor. Had something dead touched the fabric which she'd wrapped about her body?

Pudding immediately went to sniff the robe, licking the pocket, and snuffling inside. She dragged something out between her teeth.

'Stop that, Pudding!' Ophelia cried, pushing the terrier away. It was then that she saw the slight red stain on the cloth and, with a horrified gasp, identified what Pudding held in her mouth: the bloody foot of a bird.

ADVICE

10AM, BOXING DAY, 1928

OPHELIA DRESSED HURRIEDLY, putting on a grey and purple tweed skirt and a matching woollen sweater in dark violet. She ran the brush swiftly through her curls and scooped up Pudding. She had no desire to linger in her room. Forces were at work that she was unable to fathom but, certainly, something, or someone, at Castle Kintochlochie wished her ill.

Ophelia needed to speak to Horatio; he alone could be relied upon not to dismiss her anxieties. Finding his room already empty, she came downstairs, to seek him out.

In the Great Hall, Enid and the Colonel were making their farewells.

'A dreadfully long drive,' Enid was saying, 'Monty has an old regimental friend near Exeter, and we'll stop at inns on the way down. It should only take three or four days.' She gave Morag a parting kiss. 'I've never been to the West Country. It's rather exciting really. Monty does so love the freedom of the road.'

Morag turned to Enid's sister. 'You're sure you won't stay longer, Marjorie? We'd enjoy having you...'.

'I'd love to, but work calls. There's always so much to do! Especially at this time of year... all those sweet little kittens and puppies turned out of homes once Christmas is over.' Marjorie raised her eyebrows apologetically.

Morag nodded. 'You know where we are, and you're always welcome.'

Several of the other guests had also breakfasted early and were gathering, making ready to depart.

'We're off to the Boxing Day Hunt, setting off from The Red Stag,' Lady Faucett-Plumbley was telling Peregrine Belton. 'Flavia's a frightfully good horse-woman. Quite fearless. Best seat in the county, some say!'

'I'm sure you're right,' said Peregrine, giving Flavia a sly wink.

Ophelia located Horatio, emerging from the breakfast room.

'Too, too early for me, really,' Horatio was lamenting, 'But I've managed a couple of sausages to fortify me for the return journey. The Reverend and his wife are dropping me off at the station.'

Ophelia felt herself tremble. It was too awful to think of Horatio going. She'd miss him terribly.

'No need to look so glum.' Horatio took Ophelia's arm. 'Morag's invited me back for a few weeks in the summer, and you might pay me a visit in London if you desire a change of scene, dearest. We might even write, although I shall have to make you promise to burn my correspondence after reading. Far too scandalous for it to fall into the wrong hands.'

Ophelia tried her hardest to laugh, but it fell rather flat.

'My dear, now I look at you, I see that you're quite out of sorts.' Horatio led her into the library, where the fire was crackling merrily. He closed the door firmly behind them.

Taking a seat, Ophelia related what had happened the night before, concentrating on the unexplainable, rather than on what had passed between her and Hamish. Horatio listened quietly, nodding every now and then. When Ophelia came to the moment at which she'd discovered the ghastly contents of her dressing gown pocket, he put his arm about her shoulder.

'Who can it be, or what, Horatio?'

'You're afraid, Ophelia?'

She nodded.

Horatio gave a shiver. 'So am I. Scared for you, I mean.'

She smiled weakly. 'And I'm not imagining these strange happenings?'

'Not at all dearest.' Horatio gave her a gentle squeeze. 'I was with you in Hector's study, remember? Something peculiar is most certainly afoot.'

He patted his knee, encouraging Pudding to jump up. 'These encounters seem designed to alarm us and, most particularly, you! It's as if someone is trying to drive you away, my dear.'

Pudding wriggled to comfy herself on Horatio's lap, four legs in the air, inviting him to stroke her tummy.

Horatio thought for a moment. 'They may see you as a London interloper, even though you're the old earl's granddaughter.'

'You think I've stirred the animosity of a castle ghost?' Ophelia's face clouded. Ghosts were known to hold grudges, weren't they? To be discontented in death, as they were in life.

'Either that, or someone has been very clever, and very devious...' Horatio hesitated, his fingers pausing in their caress of Pudding's belly.

'Whether it's a ghost or a person, they're doing a jolly good job of spooking me!' Despite the fire, Ophelia suddenly felt cold. She slipped her shoes off, tucking her feet under, and hugging herself. Her grandmother had been marvellous, but what did she know of others' feelings towards her? She pictured them standing around the tree on Christmas Eve. Had someone been secretly ill-wishing her?

'Perhaps it's just as well I'm leaving soon. I've said I'll go with my parents, to London for a while.'

Horatio's eyebrows rose.

'You're letting the ghostly apparition drive you away from your ancestral home?' Horatio looked stern. 'I thought better of you, Ophelia.'

'It's not just that. Not that at all really... although, after this latest business, I think I'd rather go sooner than later. I'm sure they'll find room for me at Achnagarry Castle; it's where my parents are headed tomorrow, for Hogmany.' She fought to keep her voice steady.

'Deary me! Things must be bad! Am I to assume that you're falling in with your mother's dastardly plan to marry you to some aristocratic half-wit and pop out eight bouncing sproglets? Not that you won't make a delightful mother, of course. You have quite a nurturing streak when you're not being bloody-minded.'

Ophelia kept silent, rising to be closer to the fire.

'I do believe there's something you're keeping from me, Ophelia.' Horatio put on his strictest voice. 'Don't tell me that you and Hamish have had a tiff and you're leaving in a fit of pique!'

Ophelia picked up the poker and gave the logs a savage poke. 'I found him in a clinch, with Felicité.'

'Oh, my dear!' Horatio gave a hollow laugh. 'Felicité is snakier than Eve and Cleopatra's vipers doing a fandango! I do hope you're not going to punish poor Hamish for what is, undoubtedly, a situation entirely of her engineering.'

Ophelia looked over her shoulder.

'You didn't see them, Horatio. If I hadn't walked in...' she shook her head. 'I don't want to think about it.'

'Well, perhaps he's not a saint,' conceded Horatio. 'But I'd bet my collection of Errol Flynn cigarette cards that he's regretting it now.'

Horatio patted Ophelia's chair, urging her to sit again. 'Besides which, Felicité and Wilberforce are leaving this morning. They're pleading a change in schedule for their Edinburgh filming, but I'm not fooled. When I saw her earlier, she had a face like thunder beneath her perfect *maquillage*. She's not used to being thwarted, and I'd say that Hamish has told her pretty plainly that he's not interested.'

'Well, I won't say I'm not pleased.' Sitting down again, Ophelia managed a smile.

'But you're still leaving?'

'I don't know what I want.' A strange heaviness remained about her heart. 'I need time away from him. Being in love is far more complicated than I realized.' She plucked at a loose thread on the cushion beneath her elbow.

'Ah! Sweet thing! It's always the way!'

Ophelia reached to take Pudding onto her own lap. 'You must write and tell me how you get on with the Beatons,' she said, making an effort to change the direction of their conversation.

She whispered into Pudding's ear. 'He'll be having a far more exciting time than us, won't he Pudding!'

'You're right, of course,' mused Horatio. 'Cecil tells me that Noel Coward and Ivor Novello are expected among the house guests for New Year, so it'll be handbags at dawn to claim possession of the pianoforte.'

Ophelia gave Horatio a teasing pinch.

'And are you going to tell Cecil how you feel?'

'How do you know I haven't already?' replied Horatio, giving her a disingenuous look. He appeared suddenly shy. 'Well, perhaps I've not yet had the courage....'

'You can't know whether someone has deep feelings for you unless you give them the opportunity to show you,' she chided. 'If you think you love him, you have to take a leap of faith, don't you think?'

'Well!' declared Horatio. 'It sounds like we both need to take the same medicine, doesn't it?'

DANGER

2PM, BOXING DAY, 1928

OPHELIA DECIDED that what she needed was some fresh air. Returning to her room, she glanced about warily. She couldn't put aside the feeling that some malevolent force was lurking. What might it do next?

Swiftly, she changed into her riding clothes. She'd go and see the new foal, and ask Murray which of the horses needed exercise, just down to the loch and back. A mist was rolling down from the hills and the sky was heavy with the promise of more snow to come; if she didn't go out now, she might lose her chance.

The moonstone ring was still sitting where she'd left it, on the dressing table. Hamish's mother had worn it; he hadn't told her much about his parents but, as far as she knew, their marriage had been a happy one. The ring had symbolized their love for one another, hadn't it? She wondered if all women had these feelings of doubt, of wondering how far the men in their life could be trusted.

She hesitated, then returned the ring to her right hand.

~

The foal gazed back as Ophelia leaned into the stall. Large eyes, framed thickly with lashes. Moonshine's mother gave her a nudge, then whickered and shook her mane.

'You've done a good job.' Ophelia held out a carrot to Esmeralda, and stroked her nose. 'No riding for a while yet, though. Stay here in the warm.'

She moved over to the next stall, where Arion, a Dapple-grey, was stabled. Eager to venture out, he came straight to Ophelia, and dipped his pale head. The smallest of the stallions, she'd ridden him several times before, although she needed a hand in mounting.

Murray, putting fresh straw in the far stall, came down to help her throw over a blanket, and lift the saddle into place.

'Go easy through the snow, M'Lady,' he warned. 'You won't be able to see where you're stepping in the deeper drifts. I'd keep to the east side of the loch, just in from the trees.' Murray tightened the girth under Arion's chest. 'Last night's frost has iced the loch but I wouldn't venture out. It won't be safe for skating or anything like that for a while yet.'

'I'll go carefully,' she promised, placing her foot in Murray's palm to take her seat.

She proceeded easily down to the water's edge, though the wind had pushed the powder deep in places. Ophelia tied her scarf closer and pulled her beret further over her ears. The mist had almost completely obscured the crags, and was moving across the icy loch in chill tendrils, drifting steadily towards the trees.

She recalled her first time on the water. Hamish had taken her, and taught her to fish. He'd been patient, as he always was.

Ophelia pulled Arion to a halt. How different everything looked. The castle, behind her, had disappeared entirely in the shifting haze.

All was still, and silent.

'Isn't it beautiful,' Ophelia whispered.

Arion snorted his own plume of white into the winter air, and stamped his foot, eager to keep moving.

She clucked her tongue to urge him on. Despite the creeping cold, the landscape was bewitching. The eternal majesty of Kintochlochie never failed to calm Ophelia; she drew strength from it.

There was a crack of twigs to her right, from somewhere within the woods.

Arion tossed his head and skittered a few steps, his hooves sliding in the fresh snow, where the bank descended into the shallows of the frozen loch.

'Woah there.' Ophelia soothed him, patting his mane and guiding the horse back onto more level ground.

Had it been a rabbit, thought Ophelia, or perhaps a deer? She leant down, endeavouring to see beneath the branches. There had been a stag on the hillside not so long ago, but they rarely grazed under the trees. The firs grew densely, and kept their foliage all winter long, making it difficult to see beyond the treeline.

From somewhere in the mist, there was the softly muffled sound of feet passing through snow, moving swiftly.

Ophelia had sought solitude, but she was not alone. Someone was approaching.

'Who's there?' she called, turning Arion about, but the fog swallowed her voice, and there was no reply.

From under the trees, again, she thought she saw something. A sweep of white, like an owl's wing, outstretched and swooping? Or the gliding arm of some phantom? Hadn't Morag mentioned a spirit said to walk by the loch: a servant girl who came to an unhappy end?

'Who's there?' Ophelia called again. The stillness of the landscape suddenly felt eerie. With all that had happened, had she been wise to come out on her own?

She might divert from the path, but she was reluctant to head into the forest. This section was due for thinning; she'd be unable to ride through easily. She might continue around the loch, but there were too many dips and rises for it to be safe. The snow could have drifted several feet deep, and she couldn't risk injuring Arion.

There was nothing for it but to face whatever was advancing. Ophelia called once more, into the rolling mist, and heard the faint echo of a returning voice, one that spoke her name.

The vapours drifted thin and she glimpsed a dark shape. Another moment, and a horse was upon her: huge and black, rearing up to avoid Arion, who whinnied in fear and pranced backwards.

'Good God!' growled the figure. 'What are you doing? The snow's coming in over the pass and this mist is as thick as soup. You've been out for over an hour. Morag's been asking after you, and no one knew where you were.'

'Hamish!' cried Ophelia, stifling a sob.

'No harm done. I've found you now.' Hamish tempered his gruffness. 'I guessed you might have been to see the foal, and Murray told me you'd ridden out. I've been looking for you for some time. Damned difficult, and not helped by you having chosen the palest coloured horse in the stable!'

Ophelia felt her face burn. She'd been so wrapped up in herself, she'd not considered telling anyone where she was going.

Hamish loosened his feet from the stirrups and slithered down.

'I've been thinking about you all morning. About us.'

He came closer, reaching one hand to Arion's nose and touching the other to Ophelia's leg.

'We must try again,' he urged. 'Don't let's lose what we have, Ophelia. I've been a fool...' He grimaced. 'I'm hot-tempered, I know. Too hasty to act at times.'

'Too impulsive,' Ophelia added.

'Perhaps.'

Ophelia took off her glove and reached down her hand to touch his.

He saw the ring. 'You're still wearing it.'

Hamish took her hand, encasing it warmly, and she felt her heartbeat quicken.

'I want you to trust me, Ophelia. I'm not saying that I won't make mistakes, but I love you.'

He looked up, earnestly.

'Your happiness is tied to my own, and I shall do everything in my power to keep harm from coming to you.'

She nodded, gulping down the lump which had come to her throat.

Hamish slid the moonstone from her finger and walked to the other side of Arion's head. Tugging off her remaining glove, Ophelia held out her left hand. He lowered his lips to her palm and held it to his cheek.

'You'll have me?'

She nodded again.

Gently, he placed the ring upon her third finger.

~

From between the trees, Hettie watched, tears welling in her eyes.

Hadn't she been clever, finding how the oak panelling slid back, in the corner of the linen cupboard? It had been quite frightening the first time, feeling her way in the dark, with only a lantern to guide her. She might not have thought of it if Susan hadn't been telling stories of when her grandmother was in service at the castle. Hettie's mother had never mentioned such a thing, although Mary, Lady Morag's maid, seemed to know something of it.

Hettie had worried that someone might come along and shut the panel behind her. She might never find her way out. But she'd been brave, hadn't she!

When she'd realized that the passage gave onto every bedroom on that floor, she'd known what she must do. It was only right wasn't it, to use her knowledge to a good end?

And fancy finding the white cloak, with its great hood, in her attic room, inside one of the trunks; there was a guiding hand in it, surely? She'd dressed up and gone to Lady Ophelia's room. She'd given someone a fright, hadn't she! Just not the right person...

She knew the passageway quite well now. Knew just where to rest her fingers to slide the panelling open. She'd even kept that blasted dog quiet, having fed it a piece of ham soaked in the sleeping powder Mrs Beesby had given her. But what good had it done?

Mr Hamish was proposing marriage. Lady Ophelia would never leave, would she, not now...?

Hettie had been so sure, when he'd kissed her on the cheek on Christmas Eve. He'd kissed the others too, but not in the same way. He'd given her such a lovely smile. His eyes sparkled. No one could smile like that and not mean it, could they?

But here he was, holding Ophelia's left hand. She knew what that meant. Perhaps he wasn't any better than other men. They made you feel special, but they let you down in the end.

~

Hamish helped Ophelia down and embraced her tightly. His kiss was so consuming that Ophelia felt as if she were no longer just herself, but part of him too. No one would come between them. Nothing would ever part them.

He drew back, laughing into her hair, and she saw that it had begun to snow again.

'Stay close, now. I'm not losing you again,' said Hamish.

As they broke apart, they saw her. A figure in white, walking out onto the frozen surface.

Ophelia stifled a shriek, for she recognized both the cloak and the pale face which turned to look at them.

'Hettie!' bellowed Hamish. 'Stop!'

There was a single, loud crack as the ice broke, and Hettie disappeared beneath the frosted crust of the loch.

'Wait here!' yelled Hamish, running down the bank.

'You can't, Hamish! It's too dangerous.'

He'd gone no more than five steps when the ice began to splinter.

She sank to her knees in the snow.

'Come back, Hamish!'

But it was too late. Hamish fell, disappearing into the icy water of the loch.

Ophelia's scream broke, over the sound of the ice giving way.

A SAD END

6PM, BOXING DAY, 1928

'WHO KNOWS what would've happened if they hadn't gone out to find Lady Ophelia!' declared Gladys, looking up from her bread and butter pudding. 'Good job my Murray was there to help. Sir Peter says he deserves a knighthood, just like what he's got!'

'I hear that Lady Ophelia was very brave, also.' Mrs Beesby looked down the kitchen table, at the faces of those under her charge. 'She'd been lying on the ice for some time when Murray and Sir Peter came along. She's a sound head; Mr Hamish wouldn't have lasted unless she'd done what she did.'

'Very true,' said Mr Haddock. 'It was her quick thinking that saved him. Although you're right, Gladys.' He nodded his head approvingly. 'Mr Hamish couldn't have kept hold of the branch she held out to him indefinitely. Murray showed a true Scotsman's courage in dragging him to safety.'

'Good job the water's not so deep in that part, and there's no current to drag you under, or he'd have been a goner!' McFinn sucked upon his spoon. 'Nasty way to go, really! Freezing to death bit by bit!'

Mrs Beesby pursed her lips and glared disapprovingly at the footman.

'Although I don't fancy drowning, neither.' McFinn's eyes darted to those about him as he lowered his voice. 'No sign of poor Hettie, apparently. Don't suppose they'll find her 'til spring now, and the ice thaws!'

There was a contemplative silence, then a flurry of speculations, broken by Mrs Beesby standing and rapping a spoon on the table.

'Enough of that talk!' She looked from face to face, then sat back in her chair, the wind suddenly seeming to have been knocked out of her.

'I blame myself. I should have seen...' She dabbed her eyes with a napkin. 'If I'd been able to get the doctor to talk to her, perhaps he'd have been able to help the poor wee girl.'

'Come, Mrs Beesby,' said the butler. 'Take a few minutes in my parlour. There are times when a small sherry is restorative.'

'Thank you, Mr Haddock.' The cook managed a smile. 'You're most kind.'

As soon as the two had departed, there was a hubbub among the staff.

'If you ask me, Hettie was a few sultanas short of an Eccles cake!' clucked Gladys. 'We all know not to go on the ice until it's been frozen a few weeks.'

'When I looked in on her with that breakfast tray, I thought there was something strange,' said Gertie. 'Her eyes were blazing something mad! I thought she must have a fever.'

'You don't feel the cold when you're caught in a fever, do you?' Susan mused, rising to collect the bowls. 'You feel hot instead. Maybe that's why she went outside; the windows don't open on them attic rooms.'

'But to go to the loch!' Bessie shook her head. 'I tell you, the kelpies called her. They lured her to her death!'

There was another silence as the staff ruminated on that thought.

Mary sighed to herself. She'd been sent to clear Hettie's room and had a fair idea of what had been playing on the young woman's mind. Between the pages of her Bible had been a note from Hamish thanking her for washing his dress shirt at short notice. There had been a pair of his cufflinks too, and a lock of hair very much the same colour as Hamish's. Goodness knows how she'd come by that. The rest of the staff didn't need to know.

Lady Morag had nodded her head quietly when Mary had told her.

Perhaps Gladys was right, and Hettie had been mad. Love could do that, couldn't it? Especially if the person you loved didn't love you in return, perhaps didn't even notice you. Had anyone really noticed Hettie? Or known her?

'Let me do that, Susan,' said Mary, going to the sink and rolling up her sleeves. 'You've washed up your fair share of plates this week. Take the drying cloth, instead. How about you tell me a story? Chores always go quicker when you're listening to a good tale.'

'Right you are,' said Susan, giving Mary a grin and passing her the big apron. 'I'll let you in on something my grandmother told me, from when she was laundry maid here, under Lord Hugo's father. Something I only ever told Hettie.'

'I'm listening,' said Mary.

A NEW BEGINNING

11.30 PM, NEW YEAR'S EVE, 1928

OPHELIA PICKED up Pudding and bent to kiss everyone goodnight: her grandmother, Constance, and then Hector, as they sat by the fire in the drawing room.

'I won't stay up until midnight if it's alright. I want to look in on Hamish before I go to sleep.'

'Of course,' said Morag, patting Ophelia's hand. 'I might go up myself. It seems wrong to be celebrating when we've had such tragedy, although it could have been worse. Thank the Lord that you and Hamish are safe. We'll have a party for you both, as soon as Hamish is recovered.' Morag looked down at the engagement ring on Ophelia's finger. 'We couldn't be happier, my dear. No matter what your mother says!'

Ophelia put more fuel on the fire in Hamish's room, and replaced the guard, in case the logs should spit.

Braveheart was usually to be found on the rug but, for the past few days, he'd not wanted to move from the bed. His head was placed across his master's feet.

Hamish had remained unconscious, waking only briefly. Ophelia placed her hand on his forehead. It was much cooler than it had been. Whatever fever had gripped him seemed to have passed.

How close she'd come to losing him. As her father and Murray had laid him out on the snow, she'd thought he might be past saving. His breathing had been so shallow, and his eyes dull. By the time they'd gotten him back to the castle, his beard and hair had been stiff with frost. It had taken several hours in a warm bath to revive him. The doctor had visited twice since then, and thought him out of danger, despite the fever.

'Sleep's the best remedy, and the body will heal itself,' Dr McBane had said. 'He's a strong man and it'll take more than this to carry him off!'

Murray had been the hero of the day, lying on the ice next to Ophelia and helping pull Hamish out. All the strength had been his, pulling up Hamish by the back of his belt, and dragging him, prone, to the shore. Thank Goodness, her father had insisted on coming out to look for her. He'd wanted to take Ophelia's place, but she'd made him stay on the bank, telling him he was too heavy for the job.

Hamish's eyes jerked open, as if from some nightmare, his fingers clutching at the bed covers. He looked about, calling Ophelia's name.

'I'm here, darling.' She grasped his hand and leaned in closer. 'I'll always be here. I'm not going anywhere.'

His voice trembled. 'Hettie? Did she...?'

Ophelia shook her head. 'I'm sorry.'

It had been Hettie, Ophelia knew, who'd menaced her. As soon as she'd seen the white cloak, Ophelia had known, although she could barely begin to comprehend the reasoning behind all that had happened. What did it matter now? It had ended horribly. Some awful melancholy had gripped her, and driven her to those acts, and then her own death.

Hamish rubbed at the ring on Ophelia's engagement finger. 'You're still sure?' He hesitated, and what he wished to say next was consumed by a fit of coughing.

'Shhh,' Ophelia soothed, laying him back against the pillows as the spasm passed. 'I won't be going back to London.' She held some water to his lips. 'I belong here, at Kintochlochie.'

Hamish smiled weakly as Ophelia smoothed back the hair from his face.

'I belong here, with you.'

Tipping off her shoes, she pulled back the edge of the coverlet, easing herself, fully clothed, under the blankets, to lie next to him. He turned on his side, resting his arm over her body, his breath warm on her cheek.

'Together,' he murmured, before he drifted into sleep again.

Ophelia allowed her own eyes to close.

It was New Year's Eve and she might have been dancing at a party, drinking champagne with the young men of wealth and status her mother was so keen to foist upon her.

Ophelia allowed herself a smile of contentment as the clock in the Great Hall chimed the twelve strokes of midnight.

She was just where she wanted to be.

READ ON...

If you've enjoyed 'Highland Christmas', you may like to purchase
the first book in the series, 'Highland Pursuits'

*Discover how 1920s debutante Lady Ophelia Finchingfield came to
Castle Kintochlochie and fell in love with Hamish.*

Look out for part three in the series, *Highland Wedding,* releasing in
late 2018.

Highland Pursuits

Refusing to marry her mother's choice of suitor, defiant debutante Lady Ophelia is banished to the Highlands of Scotland.

In her ancestral home of Castle Kintochlochie, she soon finds herself attracted to the wildly unsuitable Hamish! A weekend party brings the arrival of a host of eccentric characters, including glamorous coquette Felicité, who has her own designs on the ruggedly attractive estate manager.

Can Ophelia avoid the dangerous attentions of French aristocrat playboy, the Comte de Montefiore, and claim Hamish for her own, alongside her rightful place in managing Castle Kintochlochie?

A 1920s romance, with a dash of wicked humour.

ABOUT THE AUTHOR

Emmanuelle de Maupassant lives with her husband
(maker of tea and fruit cake)
and her hairy pudding terrier
(connoisseur of squeaky toys and bacon treats).

You can find her on Twitter and Facebook
Send her a hello. Tag her in a review.
Give her a wave, and she'll wave back.

www.emmanuelledemaupassant.com

BONUS MATERIAL

AN EXTRACT FROM 'BABY LOVE'

8 months pregnant and still sexy!

Baby Love

Delphine's rat-fink husband has packed his bags and abandoned her for the charms of their neighbour, leaving Delphine struggling to cope. Her sisters insist that the best remedy for a broken heart is

a dose of pampering. Cue a spa break, where handsome Texan Jack
and suave Marco await.
Will there be more in store for Delphine than a hot stone massage
and a spell in the Jacuzzi?

A romantic comedy from Emmanuelle de Maupassant, set in
British Cornwall.

Prologue

Here is the story of how you came into being.

A caravan holiday to Dorset. A beautiful spot, just above
Durdle Door, along from Lulworth Cove. Lovely.

It would have been lovely, if it hadn't been raining. Continuous
rain. Sheets of it. So much rain that you couldn't see the beach, or
the crashing, rolling waves, or famous golden limestone arch
standing out from the cliffs.

What could we see? Muddy grass, and fat droplets against
misted windows.

What does one do, stuck in a tiny caravan, in unseasonal
weather? One drinks tea, and plays Scrabble. And one shags.

We finished a 160-pack of teabags. We played seventeen games
of Scrabble. And we shagged. A lot.

Bingo. Conception.

No mean feat, as we'd been trying, off and on, for about six
years. I'd given up thinking about it. We hadn't mentioned parent-
hood for months. A baby, it seemed, was not on the cards.

But, at last, you decided to come along.

∼

It's 5.30am and I'm awake. In fact, I've been awake for most of the night. There's only one thing to do when you, 'the bump', refuse to let me sleep: make a good, strong cup of tea, open a packet of chocolate digestives and log into Facebook.

Although I know I shouldn't (I really, really shouldn't), I can't resist opening 'his' page, Adam. When I do, it's filled with pictures of him with 'her'.

The new 'her'.

A 'her' who's not almost eight months pregnant: Maria, our next-door neighbour.

Am sitting up in bed, laptop balanced on my impossibly inflated belly, reaching past my impossibly inflated tits, torturing myself with his photographic catalogue of loved-up bliss.

There's a heavy, squashed feeling at the bridge of my nose. The tears want to come, but I won't let them.

Instead, I'll eat another biscuit. Fuel my anger with some sugar. You wriggle in approval. Chocolate digestives are our favourite.

Have spent the past couple of days fielding phone calls from 'so-called' friends. Not true friends, but acquaintances wishing to gloat. Well-known fact that women of St. Ives miffed at Adam having married me instead of them, and have been secretly waiting for us to split up.

Now, news of sexually incontinent husband has swept town, and vultures are picking over corpse of our marriage.

Have told them that all a misunderstanding and rumours are heinous gossip. Have even defended Adam, saying has been under strain from imminent fatherhood. I refuse to cry, despite utter humiliation.

Adam clearly having mid-life crisis, or may have brain tumour, causing him to make inexplicable decisions. Actually, this seems like most plausible explanation. Will take him to doctor's and insist on MRI. All my fault. Should have spotted signs earlier.

~

It was mid-summer by the time I realized you were on the way. I didn't twig that my period hadn't arrived until well into the second month. It was the queasiness that alerted me. That and my cup size almost doubling overnight.

Adam had a rare evening off, and we were sitting on our little balcony, drinking wine and eating posh crisps, listening to waves lapping against the harbour wall. We'd just started the inevitable game of Scrabble.

He nipped to the loo and, while he was gone, I rifled through the letters bag, to spell out a message on the board.

'WE R HAFING A BABY'

Some of the letters refused to make themselves known. I did my best.

I'd been waiting to tell him, wondering how to break this momentous, life-changing news. It seemed too important to just blurt out. I seized the moment.

'What the fuck!' I believe he said.

'That's supposed to be a 'V',' I explained.

'I can see what it says,' said Adam, and he wasn't smiling.

I'd been expecting whoops of delight, followed by tears of joy, followed by a dash to buy champagne. I'd expected declarations that Adam would be the best dad in the world, ever, and that we must phone everyone with the amazing news.

Clearly, I'd misjudged the situation.

'I thought we'd given up on all that malarkey,' said Adam stonily.

I felt my lip quiver.

'I had, really, given up hoping. I thought it would never happen. It was Durdle Door that did it. Dorset magic.'

He didn't laugh.

'I'm going out.'

He slammed the door.

It was 2am before he came back.

~

It used to be me and Adam against the world: fresh out of university, and penniless, but who needs money when you have love? Then, I set up my business, designing and maintaining websites. It did well quickly, and we were no longer scraping by. Not too long after, a legacy split between my sisters and myself, from my grandmother's estate, was enough for me to buy the upper floor flat in a house in St. Ives.

Bijou, as the property agents say. Really, just a bedroom, galley kitchen, and living room. Cosy though: full of rugs and cushions and with two deep sofas. When the fire's lit, you feel as if you never want to leave.

From the back windows, you can see the harbour: perpetual seagulls and holidaymakers, ice-creams and Cornish pasties. Idyllic.

It's perfectly placed for all the delights of a thriving seaside town. It's only occasionally that you're woken at midnight by drunken men vomiting on the pavement below the bedroom window. That, and the odd playful wrestling match, punctuated by manly grunting.

Adam took a job at one of the seafront pubs. Not many openings for geography graduates; plenty for barmen, especially those who are charming, and suavely handsome. It wasn't long before he was appointed manager.

He loved it. So much, in fact, that he worked from lunchtime right through until closing most days. Or so I thought. He could tell me anything, and I believed it. I'd be at home, busily tapping away on my computer.

Next door, it turns out, Adam was busy too: applying himself to giving Maria multiple orgasms.

Maria may be older enough to be his mother but she's far from matronly. Whatever it is that attracts men, she oozes it. She smiles, and men's tongues flop out. They are drawn irresistibly into her orbit, their willies leading them towards her like divining sticks, or the arrow on a compass: twirling about before finding North.

~

Silly woman! Didn't I rumble what was going on?

Perhaps, but I was living in a bubble of pregnant bliss, thinking of nothing but cots and booties, and frilly baby hats, and whether I'd be courageous enough to get my baps out in coffee shops to feed you. Adam was a natural flirt, surrounded by women at the bar. It didn't mean that he was having carnal relations with them all. Marriage is built on trust, isn't it?

Besides which, he was still having quite a lot of sex with me, which rather threw me off the scent. In the bedroom, we've always been compatible. Our shag-drives (set somewhere between cosmic and very keen indeed) are well-matched.

Being pregnant only increased my desire. Hardly a day went by without a good bonk. I considered myself a fortunate woman.

It didn't occur to me that my husband might be knocking off our fifty-four year old neighbour, then coming home to give me the same.

Fair enough, there was a bit less adventure involved. We were more likely to be arguing over who'd left toast crumbs on the kitchen worktops than shagging on them.

But Adam was getting his oats.

He was well-catered for in the conjugal department.

His sausage had plenty of opportunity to dip in the sauce.

You get the idea.

It was true that our conversation had moved on from where Adam was going to do me, and how, and with the aid of which kitchen implements (who doesn't like the occasional smack on the bottom with a wooden spoon?). We had a lot more discussions about whose turn it was to clean the grill pan, whether we should regrout the bathroom, and which type of bin bags to buy. You might say, we'd strayed from full-on dirty desire.

Nevertheless, we were having a lot more nookie than I'm led to believe is usual among couples who've a) been together for nigh on eight years, and b) are negotiating the terrain of a huge pregnant belly.

Following my Scrabble revelation, I'd avoided bringing up the baby situation, and Adam hadn't mentioned it, as if, by ignoring the fact, it might go away. Each time I suggested a trip to Truro to purchase 'baby things', Adam made some excuse.

He's never liked shopping, I told myself. *No man is perfect.*

I was living in a delightful pregnancy love-in, cocooned in my own version of reality: one featuring midnight feasts of sausage and custard (both types of sausage).

I spent an inordinate amount of time on the loo (partially because I was constipated, but mostly because I needed to urinate every twenty minutes). I took a lot of naps, and gradually moved into the proper, big-bump clothing. I revelled in all the traditions of pregnancy, even the nausea, which gave me carte blanche to eat gingersnaps with every cuppa.

How many hours did I spend admiring my belly in the mirror? I loved my stretchy jersey dresses, hugging every inch of swelling evidence that you, ten fingers and ten toes, were growing.

Whatever madness is supposed to overtake pregnant women, I was in the midst of it.

∾

How did I find out? Did I hear, through the wall, Maria crying out Adam's name in the throes of passion?

No.

Did I find a credit card statement revealing the purchase of saucy lingerie which never made its way into my drawer?

No.

Yet again, we were playing Scrabble.

It was two days after Christmas, in the middle of the afternoon, and we were making headway on a large tin of chocolate brazils.

I popped one in my mouth, and laid the word 'climax' with the 'X' on a triple score. I gave Adam a nudge. Back in the Dorset caravan, it was the rude words that had got us going. We'd wink and giggle, and I'd soon be on my back, or bent over the table, or panting happily with my nose pressed up against the sink.

As I say, we'd been enjoying a lively sex life, regardless of the bump and my husband's off-hand attitude towards imminent fatherhood.

However, Adam didn't take the bait.

In fact, he'd been decidedly gloomy for the past week. Admittedly, he'd been working hard at the pub. It was always a busy time, the Christmas period. And he'd endured the 25th in the company of my parents and two older sisters, Juliet and Suzanne, plus Suze's husband, Nigel, and four young children. It was enough to make anyone desperate.

My parents had made an inordinate fuss of me, refusing to let me lift a finger to cook anything. They wouldn't allow me so much as to make a pot of tea. I had the best armchair and everything. Even the dog was jealous.

Adam ended up in the kitchen with my dad, peeling seven kilos of potatoes and five of carrots and parsnips.

'Triple X,' I said, nudging him again, and winking.

'Hmmm,' said Adam.

And then he said it.

'Delphine, I don't think I'm happy anymore.'

'No worries,' I replied. 'We don't have to play Scrabble. There's Pictionary and Monopoly in the cupboard.'

'It's not the Scrabble,' he said.

'Do you fancy a walk?' I offered. I was cosy inside. More than content to snuggle down with a hot drink and a blanket. Outside was cold, and blustery. However, I'm all for give and take. Regardless of having to waddle, I'd get wrapped up and brave the outdoors, if it made Adam happy.

'We need to talk,' said Adam.

The face he presented to me wasn't that of my loving husband. It wasn't even that of a husband who quite likes you really but is mildly miffed at something you've said or done. It was the face of someone who wants to say something awful, and who has detached all the warmer emotions, in order to go through with it.

'You're scaring me, Adam. What's the matter? Are you ill? What's happened.'

I reached out to touch his arm, but he pulled away.

'I should have spoken sooner, but there was Christmas... I've not been happy for a long time. We're only in our late thirties but we're like a couple of old-age pensioners.'

'We really don't have to play Scrabble,' I argued.

'It's not the bloody Scrabble!'

Adam never raised his voice. He was a calm person. But here he was, the decibels definitely louder than usual.

'We used to have a good time, even when we didn't have any cash. We'd be out and about, meeting up with friends: bonfires on the beach, camping, surfing, all that. We hiked around Central Asia three years ago. You've become like some old granny since you got pregnant. You're even knitting for God's sake.'

I honestly couldn't think what to say. I looked down at my bump and I looked back at him. It was true that I'd recently begun knitting a baby blanket (very badly). I hadn't been aware that it was a punishable offence.

'I'll go and strap on my roller skates, shall I?'

'It's too late for that,' he replied, rather missing the sarcasm. 'You've just become boring. Not your fault maybe, but it's true Delphine. You're not the woman I married.'

I opened my mouth to reply, but, in truth, words failed me.

He carried on with 'the speech'.

'You may be content sitting in, pottering about, and doing middle-aged stuff, but I'm not. I want to live a little.'

Despite the injustice of what he was saying, and the utter hurtfulness of it, I began to plead, summoning the calmest voice possible.

'Once we've had the baby, we can make more of an effort: go for hikes along the cliffs with one of those baby-carriers on your back. You can surf, and we'll watch and cheer you on. I'll bring a picnic and a thermos of tea. It'll be great.'

'You're not listening, Delphine.'

His voice took on a horrible hard edge; one I'd not heard before.

'I don't want to be married anymore. I want to pursue my own happiness.'

Everything slowed down, my thoughts dragging. The man I love, it appeared, was no longer in love with me. It wasn't just a stab to the heart, it was an ice-pick bludgeon. I had become no more than a nuisance.

And you too, my little bundle, nestling somewhere beneath my ribs; you, also, were no more than a nuisance.

It was like *Invasion of the Body Snatchers*. My Adam was no longer in there. His eyes were dead. He'd been replaced by a horrible, emotionless automaton. Or an alien (as it turned out, one that wanted to shag our floozy neighbour).

I sobbed. I pleaded. If prostrating myself on the floor would've changed his mind, I'd have done so.

His jaw only clenched in resolve.

'I knew you'd be like this,' he said at last. 'It's why I kept putting it off.'

Something else came into his expression then: distaste. And seeing that changed something in me too. My panic and heartbreak shifted, and anger flared in their place.

'I'm sorry this is so inconvenient and unpleasant for you,' I snapped. 'Far be it from me to stand in your way. Don't worry about the vows you made on our wedding day, or the fact that you're going to become a father in two months' time. Just go and enjoy yourself.'

I watched, incredulous, as Adam got up and went through to the bedroom. He returned half a minute later. I wondered when he'd packed the bag he was holding. A day ago, or a week...

'That's it then, is it?' I said. 'You're off.'

He shrugged and walked to the door.

'I'll be in touch.'

'Wait! Adam, where are you staying? Where will you be?'

I had to ask. I needed to know. I couldn't just let him walk out the door.

Adam looked back over his shoulder. For a few moments, he must have wrestled with telling me the truth. He hesitated. He'd been telling me lies, of various sorts, for months. What would another one have mattered?

But he didn't tell me a lie. Among all the deceit, he decided to tell me something that was the truth.

'I'll be next door,' he said. 'With Maria.'

I grabbed the nearest thing, a snow globe from the Isle of Wight that we'd picked up on holiday the previous summer, and flung it.

I wasn't fast enough. He dodged through the door and was gone. The globe shattered as it hit the wall, sending fragments in all directions.

Want to read more?

Download your gift copy of 'Baby Love' free - from Amazon

MORE FROM EMMANUELLE DE MAUPASSANT

READ ON, for details of other works by Emmanuelle de Maupassant, including her latest release, set in the late 1940s, *Dorchadas House.*

Yearning for new surrounds, Iris Muir accepts a position at

historic Dorchadas House, on the remote Scottish island of Eirig. Drawn to the wild landscape, Iris hopes to forget the burdens of her past: her father's death, a narrow life in a small-minded town.

But the dilapidated manor houses its own secrets. There are strange cries in the night, and is the stoic housekeeper Mrs McInnes all she seems? Iris begins to have disturbing dreams about the maze, planted centuries ago in the manor grounds to honour the 'old ways', concealing something even older.

"Even on that first night, I dreamt. A presence, in the darkness."

Despite the consuming task of refurbishing the manor as a guesthouse, Iris increasingly feels the brooding presence of Neas and Eachinn, the two brutish farmhands who seem as much a part of Dorchadas House as the old maze.

As autumn wanes and Samhain Eve approaches, the island folk prepare to honour the dead and the Goddess Nicneven, as they have done for generations past.

"The women play their part, too. We're the most important, you could say ..."

Has something more than chance drawn her to Eirig?

Dorchadas House is now available from Amazon

MORE FROM EMMANUELLE DE MAUPASSANT

A dark romance series, set at the turn of the old and new centuries, in the late Victorian age.

The Gentlemen's Club

A place where no desire is forbidden; where no hunger is taboo.
Lady Maud Finchingfield is eager to follow a path of self-determination, struggling against the social constraints placed upon her as a young woman in a man's world. Meanwhile, Lord

McCaulay falls under the spell of Mademoiselle Noire, the hostess at his exclusive London club. Despite suffering humiliation at her hands, he is drawn into her web, entering a spiral of obsession. Can each player in the tale avoid scandal, as they embark upon a series of dangerous choices?
Recommended by Stylist magazine as 'a mind-blowing' read.

Italian Sonata
What dark secrets lie within those walls? Madness, abduction, imprisonment... murder? The past does not lie quietly.
Towering above its island of wave-lashed rock is Castello di Scogliera. Look up at the narrow windows, and you might think yourself watched. Something, or someone, has been waiting for Lady McCaulay to arrive...
A sumptuous Gothic Romance, filled with mystery, intrigue, and the lure of the sensuous.

The third installment in the Noire series is due for release in early 2019

MORE FROM EMMANUELLE DE MAUPASSANT

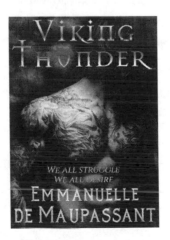

We all struggle. We all desire.

Viking Thunder

Captured. Seduced. Craved.

Eirik is used to taking whatever he desires for his own, and what he wants is Elswyth. He'll have her submission, even if it means parading her in front of his drunken raiders and threatening to claim her before them all.

Elswyth has gone from a loveless marriage to the captive of a Viking brute. So why does she find herself aroused and yearning to submit to his fierce seduction?
Her heart speaks to his hardened soul and he vows to show her the true nature of what it means to be loved by a Viking.

In Eirik's arms, can Elswyth find what her heart yearns for? Dare she follow him to distant lands, across the vast, dark sea?

Short stories by Emmanuelle de Maupassant appear in the following anthologies
Best Women's Erotica of the Year Volume 3 (Cleis Press)
Big Book of Submission Volume 2 (Cleis Press)
For the Men (Stupid Fish Productions)
Dirty 30 Volume 2 (Stupid Fish Productions)
Amorous Congress (Riverdale Avenue Books)

ABOUT THE EDITOR

Adrea is a Melbourne-based freelance writer, editor and former stage director. She holds a BA (Hons) in theatre studies. Through her fiction and non-fiction writing, she engages with themes of the feminine, often focusing her lens on the rich diversity of feminine sexuality. She is also deeply interested in myth and fairy tale re-tellings.

After many years interpreting play-texts as a theatre director, Adrea is now applying those skills in deepening the "theatre on the page", and enhancing the writer's voice through developmental editing. She has assisted authors with over thirty short stories and various long-form works over the last few years, including several by Emmanuelle de Maupassant.

Adrea's erotic short stories and poetry and have appeared in various anthologies, including *The Big Book of Submission Volume 2 (2017)*, *For the Men (2016)*, *Coming Together: In Verse* (2015) and *Licked* (House of Erotica 2015), *The Mammoth Book of Best New Erotica 13*, and in *A Storytelling of Ravens* (Little Raven 2014). Her provocative flash fiction and short stories have also featured on many online sites. In another guise, she has published a feminist creative essay in *Etchings* literary journal (2013), and her short memoir story was published in an Australian anthology the same year. Currently, Adrea is working on her first collection of themed erotic short stories ***Watching You Watching Me*** and her first novella, a mythical re-telling.

To discover more, visit her at:
    https://koredesires.wordpress.com/about/
    https://www.facebook.com/adrea.kore
    https://twitter.com/adrea_kore

36267617R00122

Made in the USA
Lexington, KY
12 April 2019